SPARKPLUG OF THE HORNETS

STEPHEN W. MEADER

SPARKPLUG
of the HORNETS

Illustrated by Don Sibley

SOUTHERN SKIES

ISBN 978-1-931177- 70-2 cloth
ISBN 978-1-931177- 71-9 paperback

Library of Congress Catalog Card Number: 53-7868

LITTLE ROCK, ARKANSAS
www.southernskies.com

SPARKPLUG OF THE HORNETS

Peewee Carson looked out the window at the weather. It was a gray morning, cloudy and cold, and the only sign of life was a sparrow that cheeped forlornly in the leafless maple tree. Peewee shivered. He was about to dive back under the warm bed covers when his mother's voice called up the stairs.

"Gregory! Time to get up!"

"Aw, Mom," he answered plaintively. "It's Thanksgiving—no school today!"

"I know that well enough. But if you aren't down to eat your breakfast soon, you won't have any appetite for the big dinner I'm cooking. Come, now—let me hear your feet on the floor!"

Peewee groaned and obediently thumped his bare

feet on the rug beside the bed. He knew it was no use trying to sleep any longer. Still in his pajamas, he sprinted into the bathroom, washed up and returned to his own room to dress. First, however, he had to do his exercises.

There was a bar rigged across one corner of the room, some seven feet above the floor. He jumped upward, grabbed the bar and hung there, wriggling his legs and loosening his joints. If the article he had read in a magazine could be believed, this sort of daily workout would soon add inches to his height. And that, more than anything else in the world, was what Peewee wanted.

After two or three minutes he dropped to the floor and backed up against the door frame, holding a ruler level across the top of his head. He made himself as tall as possible, but conscientiously tried to keep his heels on the floor. When the end of the ruler was planted against the frame he turned hopefully to look at its under-edge.

What he saw was disappointing. It rested exactly where it had for a month—at the pencil line that marked five feet, three inches. With a sigh he pulled on his clothes and went down to breakfast.

The kitchen was full of warmth and bustle and tantalizing odors. Mrs. Carson was stuffing the turkey. Peewee's older sister Jane was rolling out pie crust, her arms flour-dusted to the elbows.

"You'll find your orange juice in the refrigerator," said his mother. "I've kept your pancakes warm on the back of the stove. Hustle, now, Son. I want you to get those leaves raked this morning."

The boy put a tablespoonful of cod liver oil in the glass of orange juice and stirred it. He made a face at the taste of the stuff but swallowed it down manfully. It was supposed to build bones and make people grow. When he had finished the concoction he poured himself a big glass of milk and tackled the pancakes, putting on plenty of butter and syrup. There was nothing wrong with Peewee's appetite. Jane sometimes teased him by saying he ate as much as a two-hundred-pound football tackle.

He tiptoed from the table and into the living room, trying to put off the leaf-raking job as long as possible. The morning paper was there. He curled up on the davenport with the comic page and was deep in Dick Tracy's latest adventure when the telephone rang in the hall. He heard Jane hurrying to answer it. Though he didn't try to follow the conversation he could tell she was talking to a man. Her "maple sugar" voice, he called it—sweet and drawling.

After she hung up she looked in at him. "Hey, Bub," she said, in tones that were back to normal. "Better get the yard cleaned up and looking nice. We're going to have company for dinner."

"Who?" he asked coldly.

"Never mind who—you'll see," she replied with a toss of her head and went back to her pie-making.

Peewee groaned. Boy friends! Jane was attractive enough, he supposed. She had had plenty of admirers back in the city but this was the first one since they had moved to Hackersville, two months ago. Now that she had a secretarial job, she was beginning to meet people and make new friends.

He put on his windbreaker jacket and went outside. From the garage he got a leaf rake and a battered old basketball. If he had to work on a holiday he meant to have some fun along with it.

One of the first things he had done when the family arrived in this little upstate town was to tack up a bottomless peach basket on the trunk of the big maple in the yard. Half his life—ever since he was seven and in the second grade—he had lived and breathed basketball. That was why he wanted so passionately to be tall.

He dropped the rake and tried a quick one-hand shot from twenty feet away. The ball rimmed the basket, hung for a second and rolled off the edge. Peewee gave a snort of disgust. His shooting eye was out and he needed practice. Ordinarily he expected to make four out of five from that distance.

To give himself an incentive for getting the raking job done, he decided he would work for ten minutes, then put in five minutes shooting baskets. He looked at his watch and went at it.

The minutes seemed to drag very slowly while he raked, but he had cleared one corner of the yard and heaped up a big mound of leaves when time was up. He laid the rake across the pile and picked up the scuffed old basketball. A fast dribble and lay-up shot from the right—then from the left. Half a dozen from the foul line. And finally a series of set shots, slow and easy, from the corners and mid-court. He went through the routine several times and found he had used up his five minutes.

In this way the morning passed pleasantly enough. Twice he paused to burn the leaves he had raked, and the fragrant smoke drifted out across the fence like a cloud of incense. There were other places along the village street where householders were burning leaves. The smoke of the bonfires hung in a gray mist, shrouding the sidewalks, and the few people who passed by were shadowy, unreal figures.

By noon Peewee not only had his raking nearly done but his shooting eye was improving. He was practicing two-hand sets from thirty feet out when he heard footfalls coming along the brick sidewalk. They paused beside the fence, but the boy was concentrating on the basket. He arched the ball true to the mark and it went through without touching.

"Nice shot," a man's voice remarked. "You do that every time?"

Peewee retrieved the ball and dribbled over toward the fence. He was a dozen feet away when he recognized the speaker through the haze of smoke. He missed his dribble and the ball rolled away. It was the Hackersville High basketball coach, Elmer Brent, who stood there smiling at him.

"Gosh, Mr. Brent!" he stammered and could say no more.

"You didn't answer my question," the lanky young man told him with a grin.

"Huh? Oh—no, sir—only about three out o' four."

The smile was gone from Brent's face. Quite evidently he thought the diminutive lad was bragging.

"I'd like to see that," he replied quietly.

Red-faced, Peewee walked back to the middle of the yard, bouncing the ball in front of him. He was trying too hard on the first one. It hit the backboard and bounced back to him. Gritting his teeth, he drew a long breath and launched another toss. This time it wobbled on the rim and went in. He had the rhythm now. The third shot was clean and so was the fourth.

From the sidewalk he heard a low whistle. "I apologize, young man," the coach called. "Didn't think you could do it. What grade are you in at school?"

Peewee came back to the fence. "Freshman in high school," he replied in embarrassment. "I know I don't look it, but I'm fourteen."

"You live here?"

"That's right. I'm Gregory Carson."

The tall young coach grinned and reached a hand across the fence. "You and I ought to get better acquainted," he said. "I'm coming to dinner at your house today. Your sister Jane invited me."

So that was it. One of Jane's boy friends. Well, Peewee thought, she was showing better sense than usual. Elmer Brent was a real man.

"Fine!" the boy said. "I've still got one pile o' leaves to burn, but I'll be in pretty soon. I guess—I mean—I know they're expecting you."

When the last of the leaves were in ashes he entered by the back door and went quietly upstairs. Dinner preparations had reached the stage where everything was cooking satisfactorily, and Mrs. Carson had joined the others in the living room. Peewee could hear their voices as he changed his clothes. He put on a clean shirt, picked out his best necktie and knotted it with more care than usual. His hair was red, thick and unruly. There was little he could do with it, but he worked it over with comb and brush, threw back his shoulders and went downstairs.

From the hall he heard his father talking. "I never followed the game much," he was saying, "until Greg started playing with a boys' club team in the midget league. I tell you those kids were good. They won the city championship two of the three years he was on the squad. Why, they even televised a couple o' their games!"

Peewee gritted his teeth. He decided he'd better get in there in a hurry, before his father made any more rash statements. But on the threshold he paused again. Coach Brent was speaking.

"Those kids play real basketball," he said. "Some of them are dead-eye shots. I remember one game I saw in the city last winter—"

"Greg led the league in point-scoring," Mr. Carson interrupted happily. "Averaged twenty-one points a game!"

Peewee burst into the room then, his face fiery red. "Holy cats, Dad!" he snorted. "You know who you're bragging to? Just the hottest play-maker in the Big Ten, is all!"

Elmer Brent's head went back in a laugh. "These Eastern youngsters think anybody from Indiana's a hot player," he said. "I did have one year at Bloomington after the war, and got into some games as a second-string guard. Most of my basketball was played in high school, back at Muncie."

Tactfully, Jane changed the subject. She asked their

guest about his service in the Navy, and soon had him talking about destroyer duty and the big base at Guam. It wasn't until they were sitting at the table and Peewee's father was carving slabs of breast meat off the turkey that the conversation swung back to basketball.

"What kind of a team do you think you'll have this year?" Mr. Carson asked.

"Hard to say," Brent replied thoughtfully. "They were pretty green last year and we barely won half our games. This season they'll be bigger and steadier. Faster, too, I hope. Of course, the thing that could wreck us is injuries or sickness. There aren't but ninety-five boys in the whole school, and most of the time it's all I can do to scrape up a squad. I figure I'll be lucky to have four men on a side for practice sessions!"

"I hear from some of the girls," Jane put in, "that the team didn't even have uniforms last year."

Brent chuckled. "That's right. They called us the Hackersville Hayseeds. The boys played in ordinary undershirts and shorts with green stripes sewed on by their mothers. No sweat suits, of course. They had to warm up in jeans and windbreakers. Another thing we have to worry about is transportation. A lot of our games are away this year and we need cars to take us."

"Hm," said Mr. Carson. "With such a small squad it wouldn't take more than about three cars. I'll talk to some of the men out at the plant. If you give us a good team we'll get the cars for you."

"I should think the boys' fathers would put up money for their uniforms," Peewee's mother remarked. "How much do they cost?"

"About fifteen dollars apiece is the cheapest we could get them," Brent answered. "Nothing very fancy, at that. You see most of the dads are small farmers and laborers. They don't have much ready cash, I'm afraid."

"I bet they'd pay half if the boys would earn the rest," Peewee suggested. "That's what we did in the Midget League."

Brent nodded. "Maybe it would work," he said. "I'd thought of something like that myself. The kids are keen enough. They really want those suits, and I'll put the idea up to them."

The look of approval he gave Peewee made the boy feel warm inside. He applied himself to the great mound of food on his plate, but his mind was busy with other things. If only he was a little taller and had a chance to make the Hackersville team, he could think of a dozen ways to earn the money for a suit. There was no grass to cut, this time of year, but there were paper routes, after-school store deliveries, baby-sitting and other odd jobs. Any boy willing to hustle ought to be able to make three or four dollars a week. He'd do it any way, Peewee decided. Money was handy to have, even if it was only for sodas, movies and Christmas presents.

Mrs. Carson beamed on Elmer Brent. He was a guest to delight the heart of a good cook, for he ate largely and with enjoyment. The meal went on and on, through pumpkin pie, mince pie, nuts and raisins and coffee for the grown-ups. Finally they rose from the table and went into the living room.

Brent turned toward Jane with a smile. "After a meal like that," he said, "I need a little exercise—a walk, for instance. Would you like to go with me?"

To Peewee's intense disgust, his sister accepted and the pair strolled away up the street. The boy helped his mother with the dishes. She didn't seem to mind the work, for her dinner had been a success.

"Such a nice young man," she remarked. "And I hope you noticed, Gregory, how polite he was about the food. That's the kind of manners I'd like you to have when you grow up."

Peewee grunted. "He sure ate plenty, if that's what you mean," he replied. "An' he got Jane out of doing dishes. Still, I guess he's all right."

He went out to the side yard and took a few half-hearted tosses at the basket, his stomach still too full for violent exercise. As he went to recover a ball that bounced near the fence, he looked up to see his sister saying good-bye to her guest at the door.

Brent came over to the fence. "Glad I had a chance

to meet you, Greg," he said. "Maybe we'll see a lot more of each other. First call for basketball players goes up on the board Monday, and I hope you'll try out for the squad."

He grinned, waved his hand and walked away, leaving Peewee standing there speechless. The boy's opinion of his sister's new beau went up a thousand per cent.

CHAPTER **2**

HACKERSVILLE HIGH stood on a little hill at the northern edge of the town. It was a ten-minute walk from Peewee's home, but he made it, that cold Monday morning, in something under five minutes, jogging along with his books under his arm. He wanted to get there early.

He dropped the books in his home room and hurried out to look at the bulletin board in the corridor. At that hour, twenty minutes before assembly, there were only half a dozen students about, and they paid no attention to the small redhead. To his disappointment there was nothing posted on the board except some old notices of long-past events. He was turning away when a thin, scholarly-looking youth with thick glasses came down the hall. Peewee recognized him as Speck Newbury, the basketball manager. He was carrying a sheet of paper and a box of thumb-tacks.

Importantly Newbury picked out the most prominent position on the board and tacked up his paper. He almost stumbled over Peewee as he backed off to study the effect.

"Watch out where you're going, Freshman," he told the smaller boy with a scowl.

Peewee waited till he had stalked away, then came closer to read the notice. "BASKETBALL," it was headed. *"First call for squad practice."*

It went on to announce that practice sessions would begin that afternoon at three-thirty, and invited all students who wanted to play to sign up on the lines below.

Peewee's hand went eagerly to the fountain pen in his pocket. Then he thought better of the impulse. Better wait, he decided, until some other names were on the paper. He wandered back to his room and tried to concentrate on the American History lesson until it was time for assembly.

Hackersville was a town of only three or four thousand and there were not more than two hundred pupils in the entire high school. It was considerably different from the crowded city schools where Peewee had gone through the grades. At first he had been inclined to turn up his nose at the modest brick building and the countrified students. But two months of it had taught him more respect.

The principal was a young man with a sense of humor who knew how to get good work out of teachers and pupils. And work was required. Elmer Brent, for example, was the manual training instructor and handled his coaching duties as a sideline. Miss Venable, Peewee's home-room teacher, not only made her English classes interesting but led the singing and had organized a five-piece band. So it went, all through the school.

But it was the boys and girls who really impressed the city youngster. He was surprised to learn that Johnny Gale, the best all-round athlete in school, was a farmer's son and got up at five every morning to do the milking. In his own class there was a boy named Jim Hoskins, whose father was a county agent, helping farmers with their crops. In two or three excursions into the country, Peewee discovered that Jim knew more about animals, trees and plants than any book could tell him. As soon as he began to realize their good points Peewee found it easy to make friends with these small-town people. He already felt at home here.

By noon there were half a dozen names signed on the basketball paper. Peewee edged through the crowd that surrounded the bulletin board and read them. Three seniors led off the list—Gino Marchetti, Ben Greenbaum and Johnny Gale. Their names were followed by the signatures of Jerry Donovan, Clem Johnson and Ray Jones.

While he stood there, Peewee saw a big, shock-headed blond come shouldering into the circle. In a sprawling hand he wrote his name beneath the others —"Joe Pulaski." One of the girls laughed.

"That's the first time I knew you could write, Joe," she said. "I thought you'd sign with a cross mark!"

The tall Polish lad chuckled. "Don't tell anybody," he replied. "I've been tryin' to keep it a secret."

The group broke up and left Peewee alone in front of the board. He glanced up and down the corridor to make sure nobody was looking, then wrote his own name at the bottom of the list and hurried home to lunch.

*　　*　　*

The high school gymnasium, like the rest of the building, looked small to Peewee. There was barely room for one basketball court. When games were played there, he had been told, they put three rows of narrow benches along each side and the rest of the spectators had to crowd onto the old-fashioned over-head running track.

More people than he had expected were standing around the gym floor when he went in that after-noon. A number of curious onlookers had come to see what kind of a squad would turn out. Coach Brent

was idly bouncing a basketball with one hand while he talked to two of the boys from last year's team. Peewee recognized them as Johnny Gale, the guard and captain, and Clem Johnson, the tall Negro center. Speck Newbury was calling off names from his list.

"Joe Pulaski," he intoned, in a voice like a train announcer's.

"Here!" Joe responded, and the young manager made a check-mark beside the name.

He adjusted his thick glasses and looked more closely.

"Who's this?" he inquired. "Gregory Carson. Anybody ever hear of Gregory Carson?"

Peewee saw Elmer Brent look his way with a reassuring nod as he stepped forward. "Here!" he shouted. His voice was changing, and though he tried to make the word sound deep and gruff it came out in a squeak.

Several of the bystanders laughed. The nearsighted Speck couldn't find him at first and the laughter increased, to the manager's annoyance.

"You!" he exclaimed, when Peewee stood right in front of him. "What's this squad going to have next—kindergarten kids?"

Peewee's face was almost as red as his hair, but he kept his mouth shut and went over to stand with the group of players. Two more boys finally volunteered to try out, and the squad was up to ten. One of the pair was his friend, Jim Hoskins. The other was a sophomore named Cooley.

"Good," said Brent. "We'll have enough for two teams when you're all here. Now if the rest of you will clear out, I want to talk things over with the candidates."

He led them over into a corner of the gym and sat down on a roll of mats. When they were gathered about him in a half-circle he began to speak.

"What I'm going to say may sound a bit crazy to some of you," he remarked. "Hackersville hasn't ever set the world afire in basketball, and there are plenty who'll tell you it never will. Too small a town. No material. And so on—you've heard all the excuses.

"Well"—he paused, studying their faces—"this year we might surprise the good people around here. It depends on you. If you want a winning team bad enough, there's a chance you might have one.

"Here's why I think so. Last year we had a so-so season. Won one more game than we lost. But you were learning, every time you played. You were hot, those last few games. And every man of that first-string five is back. You're older, bigger, more experienced. You've played together enough so that you know what to do with the ball. You're a *team*—or will be, with a couple of weeks of practice.

"Now get this. I don't want any of you telling it around town that I say we've got a winner this year. All I've said is that if every man on the squad is willing to work like a dog—and if we get our share of the breaks—there's a chance of a pretty good season. Let's keep it a secret. Let's talk small and do our bragging with shots in the basket. Everybody understand?"

They nodded soberly, knowing he meant what he said, and Brent sprang to his feet.

"All right," he ordered. "Let's play ball."

He went under the nearest basket and started feeding them lay-ups. One by one they raced in, took the ball and jumped. Something less than half the shots went in.

"Round again and keep it up—faster!"

Peewee knew he was trying too hard. He relaxed a little, waiting his next turn, timed the catch and the jump, and hit the right angle on the backboard. The ball bounced through.

"Attaboy, Peewee!" called Jim Hoskins, and the others laughed. Peewee had hoped he could start with another nickname but he knew he was stuck with it now. He grinned and trotted back to his place.

The shooting improved as they continued practicing. Clem Johnson, the six-foot-three center, hardly ever missed one. He moved with the easy grace of a big cat, and with his height and long arms he could practically drop the ball through the hoop from either side. Joe Pulaski was nearly as tall but he lacked Johnson's smoothness. In fact, Peewee observed, there was only one man on the squad who could challenge the big center at lay-up shots. That was Jerry Donovan, one of the regular forwards. He was only five-eight in height and couldn't have weighed more than a hundred and thirty pounds. But he was fast on his feet and always moving. His left-handed drop shots were beauties.

After a while they moved out to try running shots from the floor. Peewee, no longer handicapped by his size, showed up better at this. He was proud when Johnny Gale gave him a word of praise after he sank a neat twenty-footer.

"You've played this game before," the captain said with a grin. "We can use an eye like that."

The practice wound up with ten minutes of passing and dribbling and a few tries from the foul line.

"Okay," Brent called. "Take a break. Tomorrow you'll all bring some kind of uniforms. How many of you would like to have regular suits this season?"

They all answered in the affirmative and with enthusiasm.

"One of the new boys on the squad," he went on, "has made a good suggestion about how to get those suits paid for."

He described Peewee's idea of dividing the cost between the boys and their fathers. "That'll mean each of you will have to find a way to earn seven-fifty. We've only got two games scheduled before Christmas, and I'd like to see the squad in uniform when we start playing again after the holidays. Think you can do it?"

They took their time answering, for every boy was trying to figure how he could earn the money.

Ray Jones looked troubled. "I can do odd jobs an' scrape up enough, I reckon," he said, "but I don't know about Paw. We've got nine kids to feed at our house. He doesn't have much cash left over when the groceries are paid for."

Brent nodded understandingly. "You go ahead and

earn your share," he replied. "I'll see that the rest is raised somewhere. Anybody else have any doubts?"

It appeared they all thought they could do it. Jerry Donovan's father was a plumber and he was sure he could make enough by helping on week-end jobs. Gino was a spare-time clerk in the fruit market and Ben Greenbaum delivered suits for the tailor shop. Johnny Gale and Clem Johnson lived on farms and both had 4-H Club projects under way.

Big Clem's white teeth showed in a grin. "My pappy gave me a litter o' pigs last spring," he told them proudly. "They're big enough to butcher right now, so I'll have no trouble raisin' the money."

As it turned out, the only member of the squad who wasn't sure how he would earn enough cash was Peewee. On his way home after practice he stopped at the newsdealer's store and asked about a paper route. Hackersville had only a weekly of its own, but most of the residents took a city daily.

The proprietor looked over his list of carriers. "There's a boy near you wants to quit," he told Peewee. "You rather deliver morning or evening?"

"Morning," said Peewee. "I'm busy after school these days."

"Okay, start tomorrow if you want. Be here at six-thirty sharp an' you can go around with the fellow that has the route now. After that you can take over."

Peewee thought he was in luck. Most routes would

cover about fifty to a hundred deliveries. At a penny a paper he figured he could make his seven-fifty in two or three weeks—anyhow before Christmas.

At home he asked his mother if he could borrow the alarm clock and explained the reason.

"You mean you're actually going to get up at six o'clock?" Mrs. Carson exclaimed. "Well, that's something new! You won't need the alarm, though. I'm up by six every morning and I'll wake you. Just be sure you get home in time for breakfast."

It was still dark when she called him on Tuesday morning. He rubbed the sleep out of his eyes, got dressed and stumbled out the door. Four or five boys stood shivering in front of the shop when he arrived, waiting for the truck that brought the papers from the city. Promptly at six-thirty it rolled up and the newsdealer began counting out copies.

"Ed Weeks," he said, "here's eighty-five for you. By the way, here's a new boy that wants to take over your route. He'll go along and help you deliver this morning."

Weeks was a slouching, pimply-faced youth, a little older than Peewee.

"You wanna buy me out?" he asked sourly.

Peewee gulped. "Buy" was a word he hadn't considered. "Maybe so," he said. "I want a paper route and I understand you're quitting."

The bigger boy's eyes narrowed as he sized up the redhead. "Cost you ten bucks," he announced.

Peewee stared at him. "I guess we can't do business," said he. "Ten dollars is a lot more'n I've got."

"You'd better decide. Today's the day I make my collections. If you want it you can start off fresh tomorrow. How much'll you give me?"

"Five dollars," said Peewee in desperation. He had three dollars saved up at home and he knew he could borrow another two from his father. But he hated to start off in debt.

"Well—okay—five dollars," Weeks agreed grudgingly. "But I want it tonight. You bring it to my house an' I'll turn over my list to you then. Come on—take an armful o' these papers an' let's go."

CHAPTER **3**

PEEWEE'S BUSINESS VENTURE didn't go too well at the
start. That first morning it took two full hours to
cover the route because of collections. The boy rushed
home and barely had time to swallow a glass of milk
before school. That evening he took five dollars to
Weeks' home. The "list" the boy gave him was half a
dozen dog-eared sheets of paper with names scrawled
in pencil, scratched out or erased, smudged almost
past recognition.

At Peewee's insistence he went over them, translat-
ing and explaining. "They're all paid up but two,"
Weeks told him, "an' I'll get their money Saturday.
The ones that take Sunday papers are marked with
an 'S' after the name."

That night on the way home Peewee invested twenty cents in a pocket-sized notebook. He hurried through his homework and set about copying the names neatly in the book, allowing plenty of space for checking off weekly collections. It took him several evenings to complete the job. Meanwhile a succession of rainy days slowed up his deliveries. Eighty-five papers were more than he could handle at once, so he had to make two trips to the news store each morning. He used an old suitcase strap over his shoulder to carry the bundle of papers, and folded each copy compactly as he went along, tossing it onto the porch or steps. Sometimes his aim was bad and he had to drag a paper out of the shrubbery.

Day after day he got home with only minutes to spare before starting to school. His mother was worried.

"Look here, Greg Carson," she scolded him, "you're not getting enough to eat to keep a bird alive. Look at you! You're losing weight an' goodness knows you can't afford to. How do you expect to grow if you don't eat right?"

That last argument made an impression. Peewee tried to make up for his skimpy breakfasts by eating more at noon, but that seemed to slow him up in basketball practice. He knew the thing he needed was a bicycle. Most of the other news carriers rode them and covered their routes in half the time it took him.

However, he had no money for even the cheapest secondhand bike, and he didn't want to ask his father for any more help.

At the end of his first week he made his collections and brought home $26.75, of which a little over $5.00 was his to keep. After repaying the two-dollar loan, he put the balance in his bureau drawer—the first installment toward his uniform.

The next morning when Mrs. Carson shook him awake her eyes were twinkling. "You'd better hustle down extra fast," she told him. "Christmas is early this year."

He dressed quickly, wondering what she meant. At

the foot of the stairs he let out a whoop. Standing in the hallway, resplendent in gleaming red and black, was a brand-new bicycle! The tag on the big wire basket in front of the handlebars told him the rest. "Merry Christmas ahead of time," it said. "To Greg from Mother and Dad."

Peewee had ridden other boys' bikes many times, so he felt perfectly at home on this one. The basket enabled him to carry all his papers at once. He quickly learned the trick of folding papers while he rode, and after a little practice he could hit the steps and porches almost as accurately as when he was afoot. As long as the snow held off he was able to get home for breakfast with nearly an hour to spare.

Every afternoon the squad practiced in the gym. Brent was concentrating on floor work now, with only a few minutes a day devoted to shooting.

"One thing we're not going to have this year," he told them, "is ragged teamwork. I'd rather see one of you miss an easy lay-up than make a bad pass. We won't have a lot of complicated plays. But the ones we do have must go as smooth as silk. Every man has got to know where he's supposed to be at the right second and be there."

After a week of practice there were still a lot of rough edges, but Peewee could see the team beginning to click. He was getting a line on the abilities of the other members of the squad while he did his best to hold his own with them.

Clem Johnson's work at center and in the pivot spot was consistently fine. If he had any faults they were due to his easy-going good nature. The big Negro boy didn't want to hurt anybody. Sometimes he would feed the ball off to an outside man when he had a good shot himself.

Jerry Donovan was just the opposite in temperament. He played the game with fierce aggressiveness and he was quick as a cat. The opposition had to be alert to keep him from stealing the ball in the middle of a march down the floor. At the same time Jerry's Irish temper was always close to the boiling point, and his hard play sometimes bordered on roughness. He was bound to draw some whistles from a strict referee.

Gino Marchetti, like Gale and Greenbaum, was in his last year. He had been playing basketball for three full seasons and fitted beautifully into a forward post on the team. Smooth was the word for Gino. He was fast, too, and he always seemed to be exactly where he was needed, gliding into the spot at just the right second. A lightning passer, he was only a fair shot, either under the basket or from outside. But on the foul line he was deadly accurate. Peewee once saw him shoot twenty-one straight fouls in practice. Next to Johnson, Gino was the tallest of the first-stringers.

He stood five-eleven and weighed something over a hundred and fifty pounds.

They called Ben Greenbaum "the brain." His quick mind was always two or three plays ahead of the opposition, and the way he could spot a weakness and take instant advantage of it was almost uncanny. Ben was a good team man and an excellent guard. When a desperation shot was needed, he could sink one from almost anywhere on the floor.

The team had speed and scoring power, but they needed a strong captain to steady them and hold them together. Johnny Gale was just such a player. A stocky five-nine, he packed a hundred and sixty-five pounds of brawn and was a rock on defense. He could run from tap-off to final whistle without tiring. And every minute he was talking it up—keeping his men on their toes. Johnny rarely worked under the basket but he constantly fed the ball to the forwards or the pivot man, and he could toss in one-handers from either side.

After those first five there was quite a gap in ability. If any of them got hurt or put out on fouls, the team was certain to be weaker, Peewee thought. Big Joe Pulaski, in spite of his size and strength, was an awkward passer. Also he was inclined to be rough. When he fought for the ball off the backboard he usually got it, but too often it cost him a foul for holding or shoving.

Ray Jones, Jack Cooley and Jim Hoskins were willing enough, but they lacked both skill and experience. Whenever the first team played as a unit they ran rings around the second-string boys. Peewee was the only one who had speed to match theirs and in the first week of practice he hardly ever got a chance to handle the ball. His team-mates seemed to think he was too small, and the passes went to somebody else.

Finally Elmer Brent called the second team over into a corner. "I know you boys are trying," he said, "but you aren't giving the first string enough competition to keep 'em warm. Let's make 'em sweat a little. You've got a kid here who can shoot. You've seen him sink some beauties. Never mind his size—feed him a few and see what happens. Next time you get the ball, work it down and try this. You, Joe, go into the slot as usual. The rest of you keep the pattern moving, as if you were trying to get the ball in to Joe. Peewee stays outside. Then, just when they're expecting a pass to the pivot, Ray flips the ball back to Peewee and Jim and Jack screen him from in front. All understood? Give it a whirl!"

The score, at the time, was 28-4. A fast break by Jerry Donovan slipped in another two-pointer, and the varsity trotted leisurely down the floor while Ray Jones tossed the ball in to Cooley on the offense. The pattern took shape around the basket with Joe in along the foul lane, gesturing and yelling for the ball.

Peewee was some thirty feet out and a little to the right. He saw Jim Hoskins flip the ball to Jones, then move closer to Jack Cooley, who was just in front of him. The pass came back on the bounce, right in his hands. He drew a quick breath, steadied himself and fired a two-hand shot that parted the cords cleanly and caught the first-string players flat-footed.

"Attaboy, Peewee!" yelled his team-mates. It was the only thing they had had to cheer about in ten minutes, and they started playing with fresh enthusiasm.

They pulled the screen play a second time and a third before the day's practice ended. As they went to the locker-room Ben Greenbaum laid a friendly hand on Peewee's head. "That's the first time anybody ever foxed me three times with the same play," he said with a grin. "It won't be so easy after this, but, boy— that was shootin'!"

* * *

The first game of the season was scheduled for December 10th, on the home floor. It was with Ferndale—a team which had beaten Hackersville by a close score the previous year. That week the tension began to mount. Brent drove the squad hard in practice, and a pair of nimble girl cheer-leaders rehearsed their cartwheels and flips on a mat in the corner of the gym.

On Friday afternoon a salesman for the uniform company parked his station wagon behind the building and came in to measure the boys for suits. He had samples of fabrics and colors and did his best to sell them his de luxe line, at $27.50. Brent talked him out of it.

"These kids are earning their own money to help pay for their uniforms," he explained. "Next year maybe we can afford something fancy, but right now the fifteen-dollar style will cover us decently and that's all we ask."

They wound up by ordering sweat pants and zipper jackets in dark green, with a broad white stripe around the chest. Included in the deal were green jerseys for the games they would play away. White would be their color on the home floor.

The salesman departed, promising to deliver the suits the following week, and the coach called the squad around him.

"Somebody's going to have to put up $150 in cash for those uniforms." He smiled. "Maybe I can do it, but I'd like to know about when I'll be paid. How are you coming with your projects?"

One by one they reported. Several of the boys, including Johnny Gale and Clem Johnson, had the full amount already. Peewee thought he would have enough after one more collection on his newspaper route. Some of the others were doubtful, but agreed to work extra hard. Ray Jones dug into his jeans and pulled out $7.50.

"Here's mine," he said. "I told you about Paw not being able to help."

Brent nodded. "All taken care of," he replied. "I put it up to the men at the Rotary luncheon, without mentioning any names, and they were glad to chip in."

The day of the Ferndale game there was no afternoon practice. Peewee went directly home from school and lay down in his room to try to take a nap. He didn't know whether he would get into the line-up, but he wanted to be fresh, just in case.

For an hour he lay there, tossing and twisting, his mind busy with plays. Finally he decided it was no use. He wasn't used to sleeping in the daytime. He got up and roamed restlessly about the house, waiting for supper.

"Why don't you read a book or a magazine?" his mother asked. "Or watch television?"

"What?" cried Peewee, aghast. "Spoil my shooting eye just before the opening game? Not me!"

"All right," she chuckled. "Then you can set the table for me. That oughtn't to do you any harm."

He ate very little at supper that night and his father kidded him about it. "You're as nervous as a cat," he told the boy. "Anybody'd think you'd never played before. Think of all those games in the Midget League —they never upset you like this."

"I know," said Peewee shortly. "They were different. This is high school basketball. Are any of you coming tonight?"

"Sure," Mr. Carson replied. "I thought I might drop over. What's game time? Eight o'clock? Maybe Jane would like to come along."

Jane colored slightly. "You go ahead, Dad," she said. "I've already got my ticket."

At seven-thirty Peewee joined the rest of the squad in the locker-room and put on his old white shorts and jersey, sox and basketball shoes. The green number sewed on the back of his jersey was 10.

"This isn't a weak team we're playing," Coach Brent told the boys. "But if you keep cool and play a good, steady game you'll beat 'em. Let's get out there and shoot some baskets."

The Ferndale team was already on the floor. They looked big and formidable in their maroon sweat suits, and they were dropping shots in with apparent ease. A small crowd of spectators filled most of the seats on the Hackersville side of the gym. As the white-clad squad trotted out the girl cheer-leaders went into action with a "Yea—Hornets—b-z-z-z-z—*team—team— team!*"

Peewee thought it was a pretty good yell, and it gave him a tingly feeling inside. He took his run at the basket and popped a lay-up through the hoop. After fifteen minutes of warm-up they were ready to go, loose and eager. Then the second-stringers went back to the bench and the referee called the starting teams to take their positions.

Clem Johnson got the tap and Jerry Donovan sprinted in for a quick score. Ferndale worked the ball down methodically and retaliated with a two-pointer thirty seconds later. From then on it seesawed, neither team getting much of a lead. At the end of the quarter the score stood 10-9 in Hackersville's favor, but two personals had been called against Donovan.

He drew another penalty for charging on the next play, and a maroon-jerseyed guard converted one shot to tie the score. Elmer Brent fidgeted on the bench. During the next time-out he urged Jerry to watch his tactics and stick to team play. For a while it seemed to work. The Irish boy stole the ball and fired it to Greenbaum, who arched a fine set shot into the basket. Johnson scored another from the pivot and Marchetti, fouled in the act of shooting, made good on both foul tries. At half-time the Hornets held a comfortable lead of 22-15.

Brent warned his charges that they would have to work to hold it. "These fellows are better than they've shown you yet," he said. "They'll come out fighting, this second half, so stay on your toes."

Before the period was a minute old, Ferndale had scored five quick points and Jerry Donovan had fouled out. With their lead cut to a bare field-goal margin, the Hackersville team buckled down to try to hold it.

But Joe Pulaski, who replaced Jerry at forward, made a wild pass under the basket. A Ferndale man grabbed the ball, scurried down on a fast break and sank the two-pointer that tied the score.

"Okay, Peewee," growled Brent. "Go in there for Joe."

CHAPTER 4

FOR A SECOND the small redhead was too surprised to move. Someone pushed him and he found himself on his feet, trotting toward the scorer's table. He still couldn't believe he had heard right when he ran out to take Joe's place in the line-up. Ray Jones was older and bigger and should have had the call.

There was a buzz of questions on the Hackersville side, and some wag in the Ferndale rooting section raised a laugh with the remark that the Hornets must be scraping the bottom of the barrel. But Peewee was too busy to notice. He had taken a pass from Ben and dribbled down the floor like a jackrabbit, sidestepping two defenders. Unbelievably, he was six feet from the basket. The long-legged Ferndale center made a lunge to stop him and hacked at his arm as he fired. But the ball was already on its way. It bounced through while the referee's whistle shrilled.

"Foul on Number Three," the official called. "The goal counts. One plus one."

Peewee steadied himself on the line and drew a couple of long, slow breaths while the players got into position. He bounced the ball once, twice, and arched his shot through the cords. The roar that filled the gym was deafening as he hustled back down the floor. The Hornets were out in front once again.

They never lost the lead after that. Ferndale, hastily revising its strategy, put two men on Peewee. As a result the four Hackersville regulars had a field day. They peppered the basket from all angles and rang up a dozen points before their opponents got another goal. In the final quarter Peewee came out and Jones replaced him. The score when the game ended was 43-30 in the Hornets' favor.

From the bench Peewee looked up to see his father and sister sitting right behind him. Mr. Carson leaned forward to slap him on the back.

"Nice going, Son!" he whispered. "You sure sparked that rally."

The words were echoed half a dozen times in the locker-room as they showered and dressed after the game.

"We got ourselves a secret weapon!" Gino chortled.

"Any time things get tough, put in Peewee. They can't even find him!"

Joe Pulaski was the only glum member of the squad. He scowled at Peewee as if the little freshman were to blame for his misfortune. Peewee wanted to give the bigger boy a word of comfort but there wasn't much he could say.

Elmer Brent left the gym early, and when Peewee got home he found the coach sitting in the living room with Jane and Mr. Carson.

"Nice going, fellow," Brent said with a grin. "I was just telling your dad you upset 'em completely with that fast goal. I think I'll save you for just such emergencies."

Peewee wasn't sure whether to be pleased or not. Once or twice he had had a sneaking hope that he might win a starting assignment. But deep inside he knew it was better for the team to keep the five regulars in as long as possible. They were good—every one of them—and they had worked together so long that they had every play down pat. It was something, at least, that the coach depended on him as a surprise replacement. Next year, with three of the veterans gone, he'd have his chance as a first-stringer.

The team was talked about, those next few days. The weekly paper carried a feature story on Coach Brent and his prospects for a creditable season. There was a flowery report of the Ferndale game which didn't mention Peewee except to misspell his name as "Garson" in the line-up column. It wound up with an urgent appeal to the townspeople to get out and support the Hornets, at home and away.

The second game was scheduled for December 17th, the Friday night before Christmas vacation. The uniforms came on Thursday. When Peewee tried his on he found the sweat pants were nearly four inches too long. The blouse was a trifle large but wearable. He hurried home after practice and asked his mother's assistance.

"Please don't cut the pants off, Ma," he told her. "Just turn 'em up inside if you can. If I grow this year I hope I'll need that extra length in the legs."

Mr. Carson was now one of the team's strongest rooters. He had talked to other officials at the new chemical plant where he worked, and rounded up three or four men who volunteered to drive the squad to out-of-town games in their cars. On Friday evening he took Jim Hoskins, Jack Cooley and Peewee in the family Buick and they set off for Denton, thirty miles away.

"How good is this team you're playing tonight?" he asked.

"Not too hot, I reckon," Jim replied. "We edged 'em out last year, an' I doubt if they're any tougher than Ferndale was. Anyhow the gang is pretty sure we can beat 'em."

Peewee had heard that kind of talk in the locker-room and it worried him a little. Back in the Midget League, he had learned that every game is a tough one until the last basket is counted.

Denton High was a much bigger school than Hackersville. There was a fine new gym with seats for more than a thousand onlookers, and most of them were filled by the time the game got under way. The squad was big, too, in numbers if not in height. Only a couple of the first team were close to the six-foot mark, but they had a rangy center who towered a good six-five.

At the opening whistle he got the jump on Clem Johnson and one of the forwards darted in past Johnny Gale for a field goal. The Hornets missed two shots, Denton took the ball and scored again, and a foul by Greenbaum allowed them to rack up a fifth point in the first minute of play.

Brent called for a time-out. "You look pretty ragged in there," he told them. "Your shooting's way off, and you're slow getting down. What's the matter? Overconfident? This team is going to beat the pants off you if you don't get rolling."

He gave Gale and Greenbaum instructions to feed Johnson in the pivot spot and sent them back in. The tongue-lashing had some effect. For the rest of the first period the team played hard and fast, and though Denton continued to sink baskets the Hornets closed the gap. They trailed by only a point, 13-12, at the quarter.

Jerry Donovan hit a hot streak in the second period.

Twice he took long passes from Clem and went down on a fast break to score. The third time he tried it he got careless with his dribble and when a Denton guard intercepted the ball Jerry lost his temper. The foul he drew for shoving was his fourth of the game.

A moment later Gino Marchetti succeeded in baiting the tall center into a foul and his penalty shot evened things up. From then until half-time the score seesawed, with only a point or two separating the two teams.

Brent didn't have much to say during the intermission. The sweating first-string men were no longer cocky about this game and he knew they would give all they had. He cautioned Donovan to keep clear of trouble, suggested a play or two and let it go at that.

As the third period dragged along, Peewee fidgeted on the bench. Jerry Donovan was playing under wraps, conscious of the fact that one more foul would put him out, and even such reliable shots as Greenbaum and Johnson seemed to have lost their touch. Little by little Denton was pulling ahead.

Brent looked over at the red-haired youngster and nodded. "Try the same fast break you pulled against Ferndale," he told him. "Then see if you can work that screen shot from outside. Go in and report on the next whistle. You'll be taking Donovan's place."

Peewee stripped off his sweat pants and stretched his legs. The next whistle came quickly. Jerry had slipped and tripped a Denton guard. It was unintentional, but the referee called a foul—Jerry's fifth and final one. With teeth clenched and eyes blinking to hide tears, the Irish boy limped slowly off the floor.

Peewee gave his name to the scorekeeper and waited for the shot. It was good. Denton 37, Hackersville 29. Peewee went down wide, whirled and saw Gale's long pass coming toward him. He jumped for it, had it, and then found another pair of arms grappling for the ball. The Denton guard tried to wrestle the ball away from him but he hung on. There was a whistle and the referee called for a jump.

The Denton player seemed to tower over Peewee like Goliath over David. A whoop of laughter went up from the stands as the pair crouched for the toss-up. Peewee's muscles tensed and he shot up as if there were steel springs in his legs. Perhaps his opponent thought he didn't need to try very hard. In any case he missed the ball and the smaller boy batted it straight into Clem Johnson's hands. The tall center pivoted with an easy motion. *Swish*—and the ball dropped through. They were only six points behind.

Clem chuckled and showed his white teeth as he patted Peewee's head on the way down the floor. Then they were in a man-to-man defense with Denton attacking. Peewee noticed that the player he was guarding liked to use a low bounce pass. He waited till the last split second, then darted into the path of the ball.

There it came, right into his hands. He was out beyond the ring of Denton men, all by himself.

Peewee heard the pound of feet right at his heels as he raced down the floor. He dribbled close to the basket but the big Denton center was there, flailing long arms to prevent a shot. Peewee pretended to lay the ball up, then flipped it to Gino, who was in position, ten feet away. The Italian boy's one-hander was perfect. They had cut the deficit to four points.

The game settled down to a tight defense and a cautious offense as far as Denton was concerned. Early in the last quarter Marchetti succeeded in getting fouled and dropped in a one-pointer, but the Denton captain came back with a long, smooth set shot a few seconds later.

Desperate, now that they trailed by five points, the Hornets fought back. But their luck was out. Twice Clem Johnson pivoted perfectly for lay-ups, only to see the ball roll around the rim and out. Denton took it off the board and came down slowly, confident of holding the lead. Then Peewee saw his chance.

They had been lobbing passes over his head, taking advantage of his small size. He waited for them to try it again and jumped into the air, touching the ball with his fingertips. Ben Greenbaum caught the deflected pass and sprinted for the opposite basket. His one-hander should have been good but again there seemed to be a fence around the hoop. Clem was there to recover. Barred from a shot, he tossed the ball back to Johnny Gale and the Hornets started to weave outside the foul circle.

"Now," cried Ben with a quick glance at Peewee. The semi-circle tightened and the little redhead kept outside, behind Johnny and Gino. Clem played his part. On the post he waved his arms, yelling for the ball. Then Ben's back-handed bounce pass flicked back to Peewee, and shooting from behind the screen set up by his team-mates, he popped it in.

The little crowd of Hackersville rooters cheered wildly as the scoreboard changed. Though it was still 39-36 in Denton's favor, the narrowing margin gave them hope.

Two minutes to play! The Hornets got the ball but their opponents kept them off balance with a pressing defense. Finally, in the waning seconds of the game, Peewee tried a thirty-footer from the corner. A Denton guard charged in viciously as he fired the ball, slamming him to the floor with his wind knocked out.

Staggering and gasping for breath he got to his feet. Surely the referee would call a foul on such an obvious misplay as that. The ball had rolled around the hoop and gone in, so that a two-shot foul might give the Hornets the lead. But they waited in vain for the announcement.

To the accompaniment of howls of rage from the Hackersville stand, Denton took the ball out under

the basket and worked it cautiously down the floor. Hardly had they got it over the center line when Pee-wee heard the long whistle that meant the game was over.

It was a dejected bunch of Hornets that gathered in the locker-room. Jerry Donovan, who had warmed the bench through the last part of the game, was mad enough to go out and fight the whole Denton crowd singlehanded. Even Johnny Gale expressed the opinion that they had been robbed of a chance to win or tie.

But Elmer Brent calmed them down. "Any referee

is entitled to make a mistake once in a while," he said. "Sometimes it's in our favor, sometimes not. You played a good game after you got going, but it was your own cockiness at the start that robbed you—not the referee's decision. Without those first few goals they made, you'd have won in a walk. Remember, you'll get another shot at Denton, the last game of the season. Save some of your righteous wrath for that one."

He paused to let the words sink in, but before they separated he had something else to tell them.

"One reason your shooting was off tonight," he said, "was lack of practice. I understand Denton has been at it since October and you've had only three and a half weeks. There won't be any school till after New Year's, but we've got a game with Red Creek coming up January sixth. How many of you are willing to work out during vacation?"

They answered him with a chorus of "I am"—"Me, too"—"Count me in, Coach."

"Good," he said. "I hoped you'd all feel that way. I've persuaded the School Board to keep a little heat on in the gym over the holidays. See you there at three o'clock Monday."

CHAPTER 5

THE ONE-POINT DEFEAT didn't make Hackersville lose interest in its basketball team. On the other hand the seething indignation that filled the townspeople was almost embarrassing to the squad. Mr. Carson's reaction was typical.

"Of all the rotten decisions!" he fumed. "That referee ought to be fired for incompetence!"

That was in the car, on the way home.

"Quit worrying about it, Dad," Peewee replied uncomfortably. "He called a good game up to that one. Maybe he just wasn't looking when it happened. And anyhow, there's no telling whether I'd have sunk the foul shots."

When the Hackersville *Clarion* came out there was

half a column about the bad officiating in the game. This time Peewee got more prominent mention for his part in the affair, and someone had checked on the correct spelling of his name. "Carson," the reporter wrote, "is proving to be a veritable ball of fire in relief. In spite of his diminutive stature he may be just the sparkplug the Hornets need to get back into their winning stride."

Peewee might have felt complacent about that tribute if it hadn't been for the phrase "diminutive stature."

"Just a shrimp," he told himself with a wry grin, "no matter how they doll it up in fancy language."

However, he didn't stay down-hearted long. It was Christmas vacation and there would be no school for two weeks. He hadn't thought much about Christmas, but now he began wondering what kind of gifts to get for his family. For once he had some money to buy them. After he made his collections that week he counted the cash in his top bureau drawer and found it came to more than twelve dollars.

Several of his customers had complimented him on the way he delivered papers. "That other boy," one of them told him, "was careless. He'd throw the paper in the shrubbery or up on the porch roof. Sometimes we never could find it. You seem to do a lot better."

They had their first real snow that week before Christmas. It drifted deep over the streets and sidewalks, and for three days Peewee couldn't use his bicycle. Still, there was plenty of time now to trudge around the route, and he didn't mind the exercise.

On one of the streets he covered every morning there was a big stone house, set back in a wide lawn. It was an imposing place, but ever since he had moved to the town it had stood silent and untenanted, its shutters closed. "The old Hacker residence," it was called by local people.

As he approached the mansion one morning, he saw two huge moving vans standing in the driveway. The shutters were open and the front door was ajar. Somebody with money must have rented the house, he thought, for it would be an expensive place to keep up.

He paused a minute to watch four men carry a grand piano up the steps, then started on, splashing through snow that had begun to melt under a warm sun.

"Hey, kid," a voice called behind him. If the hail was meant for him, Peewee paid no attention. He didn't like the words or the commanding tone.

"Hey, you—paper boy!"

Reluctantly Peewee turned. On the porch of the big house a boy of sixteen or seventeen was standing. He was a tall, good-looking lad with wavy, dark hair, wearing a sport jacket of leather and tweed.

"Yes?" Peewee asked.

"We want the paper delivered, mornings and Sundays," the new boy told him. "Got an extra copy with you?"

"No," said Peewee shortly. "These are for my customers. But I'll bring one tomorrow. What's the name?"

"Sedgely," the other lad replied. "I'll give you a quarter for one of those papers. Save me a trip downtown."

Peewee shook his head. "Sorry," he said, and went on his way.

At supper that night he mentioned the fact that there were new people moving into the Hacker mansion. "Rich folks, I guess," he added. "There was some nice furniture in the van, and I saw 'em taking in a grand piano."

"That must be the new general manager at our plant," his father answered. "I met him today. His name's Sedgely and he comes from California. He's got a son who'll be going to high school here. Pretty good basketball player, his father says."

Peewee took the news without great enthusiasm. "That's good," he said. "We could use more players, all right. I hope he fits in."

It was sunny and pleasant next morning and most of the snow had disappeared. Peewee was able to use his bicycle again. As he rode up to the big stone house he saw a woman in a fur coat and galoshes standing on the lawn, looking at the shrubbery. He dismounted and took a folded paper up the drive.

"Mrs. Sedgely?" he asked, touching his cap.

She was a very pretty woman and her smile was friendly.

"That's right," she said. "You must be the paper boy. Thornton said he'd ordered the paper delivered. Should I pay you now?"

"No, ma'am," Peewee replied. "I collect on Tuesdays. You won't mind my riding in the driveway, will you? It's a long throw from the street."

The lady laughed. "Not a bit," she told him. "And I'll have the money waiting for you next Tuesday."

Peewee hesitated. "I—I heard your son plays basketball," he managed to say. "The squad practices every day in the gym. Do you s'pose he'd like to come over this afternoon?"

"Why, I'm sure he would," Mrs. Sedgely answered. She looked at the small redhead quizzically. "Don't tell me you're on the team," she said, with a twinkle that took the sting out of the remark.

Peewee flushed. "Not a regular," he explained. "We're pretty short of subs, so I get in once in a while."

"That's nice," she told him kindly. "And I'm sure you play well, too. I'll tell Thornton, and I expect he'll come to practice."

Peewee got to the gym early that day. He found the

coach in his little office next to the locker-room, and told him briefly about the new boy in town.

"I don't know how good he is," he said, "but he's tall—around six feet—and his dad claims he's played a lot out on the Coast. I invited him to practice. Hope it's all right, Mr. Brent."

"Glad you did," the coach told him. "I heard a rumor about the boy, too, but I didn't know he'd arrived yet. What's the name—Sedgely? I'll call him up right now and make it official."

The squad was in uniform and working out under the baskets when the young newcomer sauntered in. They all stopped and turned to stare at him. Unconcerned, he walked over to Elmer Brent, hands in the pockets of his handsome jacket.

"I'm Thornton Sedgely," he announced. "You wanted to see me?"

The coach grinned. "Sure," he replied. "Glad to meet you, Thornton. I hear you'll be in school after the holidays. Want to toss a few?"

They shook hands. "Don't mind if I do," said the tall youngster. "I left a suit outside in the convertible. I'll be with you as soon as I change."

"Who's he?" asked Gino Marchetti, when the boy had gone. "Outside o' being the answer to a maiden's prayer, I mean."

Brent didn't laugh at the joke. "Maybe he's the answer to what we need on this squad," he replied. "From what I hear he was considered pretty good out in California. It won't hurt if he makes some of you hustle for your jobs."

Ten minutes later Sedgely reappeared. He wore new basketball shoes and dazzling nylon trunks, and there was a big "S.G." emblazoned on the front of his jersey.

Elmer Brent introduced him to the squad, one by one. "We'll be down at this end, working out some plays," said the coach. "Here's a ball if you want to warm up at the other basket."

The tall boy took the ball, bounced it once or twice and dribbled smoothly toward the other end of the floor.

"Okay, gang," said Brent crisply, "let's try that give and go again. Clem, you're in the slot. Work it in from the corner, Jerry, then flip back to Ben and go under fast."

They went through the play several times, with the second-stringers trying to block it. Peewee did his best to concentrate on his assignment, but he couldn't help an occasional glance down-floor. Sedgely handled the ball well, and his shots seemed to be going in. Once the younger boy saw him lope toward the basket, jump into the air and toss a clean one-hander through the hoop from twenty feet away. It was a beautiful shot, different from anything he had ever seen.

Jim Hoskins had been watching, too. "Good gravy!" he murmured. "Where'd he get that one?"

A few minutes later Brent blew his whistle. "Take a break," he told the squad. Then, turning toward the opposite basket, he beckoned to Sedgely.

"How do you feel?" he asked. "Ready to go?"

"I guess so," the tall lad replied. "I'm a bit out of practice, though. Haven't played since last spring."

"What does the 'S.G.' stand for?" the coach inquired.

"San Gabriel," said Sedgely. "It's a little school near

Los Angeles. We had a pretty good team, though."

"What position did you play?"

"Guard, mostly. I went in at center once in a while, too. We won the championship in our class last year," he added casually.

"Fine," said Brent. "I'll try you out at guard. Take Cooley's place, and we'll start with a center jump."

They lined up and the coach tossed the ball in the air. For once, Joe Pulaski got the tap. It went to Ray

Jones, who crossed the center line, then passed to Sedgely. The young Californian sidestepped Johnny Gale and dribbled quickly down the sideline. Greenbaum and Marchetti were on him at once, and Pulaski, in the pivot spot, yelled frantically for the ball. But instead of getting rid of it, Sedgely circled and jumped. The ball left his right hand, arched toward the backboard and bounced off into Clem Johnson's waiting hands. There was a long toss to Jerry Donovan and the first team had a basket.

Brent's whistle stopped the play. "Nice try, Thornton," he remarked. "But that's not the way we do it here. Joe was wide open for a pass and they had you pretty well covered."

Sedgely smiled. "Okay," he said. "After this I'll pass. I just thought you wanted to see me shoot."

"I saw you shoot while you were practicing," the coach replied crisply. "You've got a good eye. What I want to know is whether you're a team player. All right —take the ball out and let's go."

The tall youngster's face was a stormy red as he held the ball in the end zone. His throw-in to Jim Hoskins was careless, but the guard recovered and came on down, bounce-passing to Peewee. The redhead darted forward as if he planned to shoot. As the defenders converged on him he flipped to Joe Pulaski, on the post, and the big center pivoted for a lay-up that scored two points.

"That's better," Brent called. "Keep going, boys."

The first team came down like a whirlwind, fairly running the reserves off their feet. But at the last second Sedgely intercepted a pass and tossed the ball back to Peewee. That was all the little forward needed. Before the opposing guards could untrack themselves, he was under the basket, popping in an easy goal.

The practice went better after that. Put on its mettle, the varsity played better basketball than it had shown for a week, while the second-stringers fought back stubbornly.

"All right, gang," said Brent after a while. "No more practices till after the big day. I'll see you Monday, and meanwhile a Merry Christmas to all of you!"

The locker-room was quieter than usual as they dressed. The customary kidding and horseplay were held in check by the presence of a stranger. Johnny Gale came over to give Sedgely a friendly welcome and comment on his equipment.

"That San Gabriel uniform is sure pretty," he told him admiringly. "Wish we could afford outfits like that, but we have to buy 'em ourselves. You'll want to give the coach your size, so he can order a green suit for you."

"I'll do that," said the new boy with a nod. "They don't look bad, really. Mother'll want to get me a fancy one, but I'll try to convince her."

There was something a trifle condescending about

his tone that rubbed Peewee the wrong way. He finished dressing and was on his way out when he heard footsteps just behind him. It was Thornton Sedgely.

"I'll give you a lift home in my car," the older boy said.

Peewee wasn't overjoyed at the offer but he could think of no good excuse for turning it down. He climbed into the shiny new cream-colored convertible and settled back on the leather cushions.

"Nice car," he remarked. "Did you say it belongs to you?"

Sedgely laughed. "Sure," he said. "Dad gave it to me on my birthday. I guess he wanted to make it up to me for moving to a hick town like this."

Peewee stiffened. "I just came here a couple o' months ago myself," he replied. "It's different from the city, all right, but I've got so I like it. Brent's a good coach and the kids at school are a swell bunch."

They drove in silence for a block or two. Then the Californian spoke again.

"Is that the whole squad?" he asked. "Those ten that were there today? We used to have thirty or forty boys out for basketball at San Gee."

"How many boys were there in high school?" Peewee countered. "Five or six hundred?"

"Yeah—about that."

"Well, we've only got ninety-five here. You'll make ninety-six. And some o' the farm kids are too busy with chores to come out for teams. I live right down here in the next block.''

Sedgely stopped in front of the Carsons' house and Peewee got out.

"Thanks," he said. "Have a good Christmas."

The other boy smiled. "I'll try," he answered. "Same to you." And with a wave of his hand he gunned the car up the street.

CHAPTER 6

PEEWEE WENT SHOPPING that evening. He bought a good briar pipe for his father and a brocade knitting bag for his mother. Jane's gift was harder to decide on. Finally he settled for a pair of fancy pink bedroom slippers with fur trimming. His purchases took all the money he had, but that didn't worry him. The next day—Christmas Eve—would be collection day on his paper route.

The morning was clear and cold, and he made an early start. It was a weekday, so most of the householders were up when he knocked at their front doors. To his surprise, one after another of his customers added a little money as a Christmas gift. Half dollars and dollar bills began to bulge his pocket. And nearly everybody gave him a cheery holiday greeting. He was feeling decidedly prosperous when he rode his bike up the drive of the Sedgelys' house.

It was Thornton who opened the door. "Hi, Peewee," the big boy said with a grin. "Come to collect, eh? How much?"

"Ten cents," said Peewee. "Two days."

Thornton's head went back in a laugh. "All that?" he asked. "Here—catch!"

The silver dollar came sailing through the air and landed in Peewee's hand. He began to count out ninety cents in change.

"Forget it," said Sedgely. "That's a tip."

Peewee set his jaw. "Thanks just the same," he replied, "but I'll wait until I've earned it."

He held out three quarters, a dime and a nickel, and when the other boy refused to accept them he laid them neatly on the floor of the porch.

"So long," he said. "See you Monday at practice."

"Hey!" Thornton called after him. "Don't get sore. That was my mother's idea. She's taken kind of a fancy to you."

Peewee turned and grinned. "She's okay with me, too," he said. "But I still can't take it. Thank her for me, will you? And I'd like to wish her a Merry Christmas!"

It was ten o'clock before he got home, and when he counted up the cash in his pocket, he had nearly fifteen dollars over and above what he owed for papers! Christmas, he decided, was a pretty nice time of year, especially if you had a lot of friends.

He helped Jane trim the tree that afternoon, then spent an hour tying up his gifts in bright Christmas paper and ribbon. In the evening the whole family went out with a group from their church to sing carols in the streets.

Somewhat to Peewee's distress they stopped in front of the old Hacker mansion and struck up *Good King Wenceslaus.* The ancient words rang out bravely in the frosty air. Before the first bar ended, the front door was flung open and Mrs. Sedgely ran out, her sweet soprano voice blending with theirs.

"Come in—come in, everybody!" she cried when the song ended. She insisted so strongly that the carolers finally trooped into the big entrance hall. There was a cheerful open fire, and a maid appeared with steaming coffee and cocoa for all.

Outside once more, in the clear, cold night, Mrs. Carson voiced her approval of the new neighbors. "I like that woman," she said. "There was no call for her to have us in, but she really wanted to do it. I hope her son's as nice as she is. Where was he, by the way?"

"He went down to the city with his father," Mr. Carson told her. "Sedgely said he had some last-minute Christmas shopping to do and he took the boy along for the ride. By the way, I'm not so sure young Thornton'll be going to school here after all. They may enter him at Brampton Prep instead."

Peewee scowled. He'd heard of Brampton. It was an expensive private school in a fashionable suburb of a neighboring city. Thornton and his convertible and his supercilious attitude would fit in beautifully down there. Oh, well—let him go. Hackersville didn't really need him.

*   *   *

Christmas or no Christmas, Peewee had his papers to deliver next morning. He stole a look at the wrapped gifts under the tree, then pulled on his coat and cap and rode down to the newsdealer's in the early dawn. By the time he had covered his route the sun was up and the household was stirring at home. He flung his last copy of the paper on the living-room table and headed for the kitchen, rubbing his hands to warm them.

"Merry Christmas, Mom! Merry Christmas, Jane!" he called. "When do we eat?"

Appetizing odors came from the cook-stove. There were sausages in the skillet and buckwheat cakes on the griddle. And by the time they were ready to serve, Mr. Carson had come downstairs.

"Smells good," he said with a grin. "Let's go! I'm anxious to see what Santa's brought me."

They had a firm family rule that breakfast must be finished and the dishes washed before any gifts were

opened. They all shared in the kitchen work that morning and soon had it done.

"All right, Greg," said Peewee's father, as they sat down in front of the tree. "You're the youngest. You go first."

He chose a big cube-shaped package from his pile and tore off the gay wrappings. As he took the cover off the box he could smell it—the wonderful smell of new top-grain leather. With a whoop of joy he pulled out a regulation basketball, a gift from his parents.

They went around the circle then, each opening a present in turn and letting the others admire it. Peewee had an impressive heap of gifts when he got through. It included a sweater, knitted for him by his sister, new shirts, gloves, wool sox, a pair of ice-skates, two or three books, ties and candy. And, of course, there was the bicycle which had been given him earlier.

"Some Christmas!" he sighed happily. "I've got to go right out an' see if this basketball bounces!"

He had on his leather jacket and was half way to the back door when he heard a sudden exclamation behind him. His father had picked up the morning paper from the table where Peewee had thrown it, and was staring at a corner of the front page.

"It's Sedgely," he said. "He and his boy cracked up last night!"

Peewee hurried to his side and read the headline:

Then he skimmed through the brief news story that followed:

James T. Sedgely, General Manager of the Alden Chemical plant, Hackersville, sustained a fractured skull and internal injuries when his car collided with a truck on Route 17 at 8:30 last night. The accident occurred 15 miles outside the city limits as the industrialist was returning to his home in Hackersville. A passing motorist rushed the injured man to St. Francis Hospital where his condition was pronounced serious.

Thornton Sedgely, his son, 17, who was driving at the time of the collision, received only minor cuts and bruises. The car, a large sedan, was completely demolished.

"Gosh!" Peewee whispered. "What a Christmas for them!"

His mother came in at that moment. "That poor Mrs. Sedgely!" she said. "It must have happened just about the time we were caroling—and she welcomed us in and seemed so happy! I suppose she's gone down to the city to be near him."

"I expect so," Mr. Carson replied. "But maybe I'd better call up—see if there's any way I can help."

A tearful maid answered the telephone. "Yes," she told him, "they got in touch with Mrs. Sedgely about one o'clock this morning and she left on the six o'clock train. There's nothing any of us can do now but wait and hope."

The news threw a cloud of gloom over the town. Mr. Sedgely was already well liked by the men at the plant, even though he'd been there only a few days. When Elmer Brent came to dinner at the Carsons' that afternoon, he, too, was quiet and sober-faced.

"I'm thinking about the boy," he said. "Young Thornton. It's pretty tough on him, because he was driving. From what I hear, the truck had stopped without pulling off the road. The tail light must have been out, because apparently they didn't see it in time—just barreled right into the rear end. It's a miracle they weren't both killed instantly."

Later, while there was still a little daylight, the coach went into the yard with Peewee to try out the new basketball. While they were passing and taking shots, Peewee brought up the Sedgely boy's name again.

"Dad says his folks had about decided to send him to Brampton Prep," he remarked. "I guess he didn't like it much here."

"That's too bad," said Brent. "For him, I mean. I honestly think we might do more here to help him, after what's happened. He's got the makings of a pretty good man, once he gets over looking down his nose at ordinary people."

"He sure could handle that ball," Peewee said. "I was hoping he'd help the team. Did you see that one-hand jump shot of his?"

The coach nodded. "California style," he said. "I remember a game we played against Stanford when they had us running in circles with that kind of shooting. It's pretty to watch."

Brent took Jane to the movies that evening, and Peewee didn't see him again until Monday's practice session. Over the weekend there was no news about Mr. Sedgely, but on Monday morning the paper carried a brief paragraph. The doctors now gave him a fifty-fifty chance to live. However, he had needed several blood transfusions, and it was certain that if he recovered he would have to spend months in the hospital. The driver of the truck was being held, pending developments.

There was little of the holiday spirit apparent in the squad when they assembled in the gym for their first post-Christmas work-out. The boys talked quietly as they dressed. Even the irrepressible Gino was sobered by the tragedy that had befallen their new neighbors. Not until they were warmed up and playing did they forget about it, and from then on the practice went well.

The coach called them into a huddle when it was over. "We've got the tough part of the schedule coming up," he said. "This week is the last chance to get ready. Six games in January, three of them away. And twice in the month we'll be playing games with only one day's rest."

He worked them hard every afternoon, right up to New Year's Eve. They were clicking, now, Peewee thought. The second team showed improvement, too, but they found it harder than ever to score on the regulars. It was only when Brent mixed them up that the practice scrimmages became more even.

School started the Monday after New Year's, and the first January game was scheduled for Wednesday night, the middle of that week. It was an out-of-town game, to be played at Red Creek, up in the coal-mining country. Red Creek was a small town, hardly bigger than Hackersville, but its high school had the reputation of turning out big, rough teams. The boys came largely from Polish and Croatian miners' families, and some of them had worked summers in the pits. They were a brawny lot.

They wound up their practice Tuesday afternoon and took their suits out of the lockers to pack them for the trip.

"I've got four cars lined up to take you," said the coach. "So there'll be plenty of room. It's a fairly long ride and we ought to start by six. Eat early tomorrow night, and don't eat too much."

At ten minutes of six Wednesday evening the Carsons had finished supper and Peewee's father had gone to get the car out. Just then the doorbell rang.

"Open it, will you, Greg?" Jane whispered. "It's probably Elmer, and I'm not fixed up yet."

She dashed upstairs while Peewee went to the door. But it wasn't the coach who stood there on the steps. It was a tall, overcoated youth with a bandage around his forehead and surgical tape across the bridge of his nose. Not until he spoke did Peewee recognize Thornton Sedgely.

"Hello," he said diffidently. "I was wondering—do you suppose you'd have room for me in your car?"

"Gosh, why—sure!" Peewee answered in some confusion. "Come on inside. I—I didn't know you were home."

The other boy hung back. "Thanks," he said, "but I'd better wait out here. I wouldn't want to scare your family with all these bandages."

Peewee took his arm and pulled him into the house. "We've all heard what happened," he said. "I know Mom would like to talk to you."

She was in the living room, smiling and sympathetic.

"You're Thornton Sedgely, aren't you?" she asked. "Gregory's spoken about you and I've met your mother. Tell me how things are."

The tall boy's shoulders sagged and his hands made a futile gesture. "I wish I knew," he told her. "They say he's got a good fighting chance. And my dad's a

76

fighter. It's pretty awful, though, to know that I—that I—"

Mrs. Carson laid a hand on his arm. "You must stop talking that way," she said gently. "Remember, you've got a job to do now, and that is to help him get well. Are you coming back to school?"

He nodded. "They said there was no point in my staying in the city. Mother's there with him. So I came back today and—well, I thought I'd sort of like to see the team play tonight."

The car horn sounded outside at that moment. Peewee picked up his bag and Mrs. Carson came to stand close to Thornton, looking up into his face.

"That's what I like to hear," she told him. "The team'll be proud to have you pulling for them."

Peewee introduced the boy to his father and they got into the rear seat. Five minutes later they had picked up Jim Hoskins and Jack Cooley and headed north, out of town. It was nearly seven-thirty when they pulled into a parking lot near the high school in Red Creek.

The gymnasium was a blaze of lights and a good-sized crowd had already gathered around the entrance. Over the door Peewee saw a huge banner, lettered crudely with red paint. "Beat the Hayseeds!" it said. A band inside was playing loudly and a little off-key.

They were the first of the Hornet squad to reach the dressing room. The rest began to arrive soon after, and one after another the boys shook hands with Sedgely. They didn't try to say more than "Hiya," or "Glad to see you," but the sincerity was there. If they were surprised at seeing him none of them showed it.

Coach Brent summed up their welcome. "You sit with us on the bench," he told the boy. "We're going to need your support."

A noisy crowd filled the gym to the rafters when they went out on the floor. The cheer given by the little Hackersville rooting section was lost in a chorus of boos and catcalls, and the booing kept up all through their pre-game practice. Peewee found it hard to take at first, but as soon as he was warmed up he forgot the noise and concentrated on the basket.

Brent got them together for a moment before the opening whistle. "Okay, gang," he said. "They can outshout us, but I don't think they can outshoot us. Go ahead out and show 'em!"

No one member of the Red Creek team was any taller than Clem Johnson, but they were all big and broad-backed. Peewee shivered when he looked at them, for they seemed to be men pitted against boys. It was only a minute or two before he got over that idea. Powerful as they were, the red-and-white jerseyed players were weak on teamwork and ball handling.

Johnny Gale took the starting tap from Clem, passed smoothly to Marchetti, and the Italian hung up a goal. Seconds later Jerry Donovan stole the ball from a Red Creek guard, flipped it to Clem, under the basket, and the tall center laid in another two-pointer. At the quarter the score was 14 to 4 in the Hornets' favor. At the half they led by 25 to 12, and the partisan crowd was angry.

The Hackersville players kept to themselves during the intermission, but they got some black looks from the other team. Almost as soon as play started again it became apparent that the game was getting out of hand. Frantic whistles by the referee and a stream of penalties failed to stop the rough tactics of the Red Creek squad. As soon as one man was put out on fouls another, just as big, took his place.

Clem Johnson was the target for much of the attack. Once, knocked down by a two-man charge under the basket, he had trouble getting up. "Twisted my knee," he told the coach.

Brent kept the tall center on the bench and sent in Pulaski. This was the kind of basketball big Joe liked, and he gave the opposition as good as he got. But meanwhile the smooth team play of the Hornets suffered. Such points as they got in the third period were on penalties, and even their foul shooting was ragged.

Finally, in the last minutes of the game, with Donovan out on fouls and all the first-stringers bruised and battered, Brent put the second team in. The score was 31 to 24.

"Keep away from 'em, Peewee," Johnny Gale panted as he came off the floor. "Don't let 'em break you in two."

Red Creek slammed in two shots within half a minute, and pressed so hard that Cooley and Hoskins could barely get the ball over the center line. A pass came to Peewee and a big, bushy-haired guard tried to wrestle it out of his arms. The referee called for a jump. The little redhead crouched, ready to make a do-or-die leap for it, but as the ball went into the air the grinning guard planted a heavy foot squarely across his toes. Getting the tap, Red Creek roared down the floor and laid up another basket to trail by a single point.

If the crowd had been noisy before it was like a madhouse now. The Hornets hung onto the ball, desperately working it into enemy territory.

"Freeze it!" somebody screamed from the bench as Peewee went by. "Half a minute to go!"

The little forward passed safely to Ray Jones, then broke clear of the tight defense. Nobody was guarding him now, for the whole Red Creek team was intent on one thing—getting that ball. He jumped up and down, waving his arms, and Joe Pulaski saw him. A high pass came sailing out of the mob of players right into his hands. He bounced the ball once, faced the basket and let fly with an arching set shot just as the red-and-white avalanche fell on him.

CHAPTER 7

WHEN PEEWEE recovered consciousness there was a ringing in his head that blurred the other noises around him. He struggled to sit up and a hand gently pushed him back. Opening his eyes he saw his father's face bending above him.

"Take it easy, Son," said the familiar voice. "You'll be all right in a minute, and we'll get you home."

"Is it—is it over?" the boy asked.

"All over, and we won. That shot of yours was good. Then Gino went in for you and shot the foul point."

Peewee began to feel better. The ringing in his head stopped and he got up shakily, his father helping him. Most of the crowd had left the gym.

Waiting for them at the entrance of the locker-room was a husky youngster in a Red Creek uniform. He thrust out a ham-like hand.

"Sorry you got hurt," he blurted, in a newly acquired bass voice. "Guess we played pretty rough. You guys are good an' I hope you win a lot o' games."

Thornton Sedgely sat beside Peewee in the car on the way home. The game had taken his mind off his own troubles and though he didn't talk much, Peewee could sense an unexpected loyalty to the Hornets in his tone.

"That Johnny Gale's a nice play-maker," he re-marked. "Steady as a rock and always where he ought to be. It's too bad the game got so dirty. I think we'd have won by twenty points."

The "we" pleased Peewee. He outlined some of the good points of other first-string players. "If only Jerry Donovan could keep his temper," he said, "he'd score as many points as anybody in the league. But he's al-ways out on fouls just when we need him most. It's too bad Clem's knee got hurt. We'll miss him bad at center if he isn't ready for the next game."

There was a moment's silence. Then the California boy spoke shyly. "I've played a little center," he said. "If the coach would let me practice with you, maybe I could help out."

Peewee felt better by the time they got home, and after a night's sleep his headache was gone. However, his mother insisted on taking him to see the doctor next morning. Dr. Edwards checked his reflexes, looked into his eyes and put him through a number of other tests.

"You're okay, Gregory," he said at last. "You had a slight concussion but the effects are about gone. Just take it easy for a few days and get plenty of rest."

The boy had a scraped knee and a bruised hip about which he said nothing. He was confident he could take care of those himself with iodine and arnica. If taking it easy meant staying out of basketball practice he had no intention of following instructions. But when he got to the gym that afternoon, the coach refused to let him dress. He sat on a pile of mats in a corner and watched the squad work out.

The second team had a brand-new forward that day. Thornton Sedgely showed up, wearing an old, stained pair of trunks and a plain athletic shirt. Bandages and all, he took part in the shooting drill, then lined up in Peewee's spot for floor practice.

It was apparent from the start that he was out to prove he could play a team game. Several times Peewee saw him pass up chances for goals and feed the ball off to one of his mates. Brent saw it too and grinned. The next time the California boy got the ball, the coach yelled, "Shoot!" Sedgely pivoted obediently and dropped in a one-hander from outside. It was a beautiful shot and everybody cheered.

Five minutes later, Brent blew his whistle and made a switch in the line-ups. With Clem Johnson injured, he had been using only four men on the first team. Pulaski had moved up to take the regular center's place and Greenbaum was bolstering the second string. Now the coach sent Sedgely in at center and brought Pulaski back to his usual second team spot.

Obviously, big Joe didn't like the move. From the first jump he crowded the new man aggressively, and in less than half a minute he had a foul called on him for hacking. Sedgely sunk it easily, but before Jim Hoskins could pass the ball in to resume play, Brent called the squad around him.

"Listen to me, boys," he said soberly. "We've got two men out with injuries. That means every one of you that's left has got to play his best and play clean. There's no room for any jealousy in a little squad like ours. You, Joe, and you, Thornton, are both going to get plenty of chances in the next couple of games. So shake on it and let's start fresh."

They shook hands, but Joe was still scowling as he pounded down the floor. With Clem Johnson out he had thought his promotion to the varsity was sure. Now this fancy-shooting newcomer was in there at center, showing him up, and the idea rankled.

After practice Peewee stayed in the locker-room while the squad dressed. Pulaski said nothing to anybody, but the others were chatting and joking as usual.

"Hey—how's about a ride in that snazzy convertible?" Gino Marchetti asked his new team-mate with a grin. "You got it here?"

Peewee saw Thornton's lips tighten. "No," he said quietly. "I'm not driving these days. I came to school on foot."

Gino looked embarrassed. "Oh," he mumbled. "Sure—I get it. Sorry."

It was dark outside when Peewee and Thornton left the gym. They turned the corner beyond the school and saw a big figure waiting under a street light. As they drew nearer Joe Pulaski planted himself squarely in their path.

"Hi, Joe," said Peewee nervously, but the Polish boy wasn't looking at him. He was glaring straight at Thornton.

"If you weren't all bandaged up," he growled, "I'd sock you one right in the nose."

Thornton grinned. "Well," he said lightly, "it's broken any way, so go ahead if it'll make you feel better."

A look of bewilderment spread across Joe's rugged face. He hadn't expected that kind of an answer. His big fists clenched, then opened again, and his hands hung loose at his sides.

"Naw," he said finally, "I don't hit sick guys." And he turned to walk away.

"Wait a minute," Thorton told him sharply. "Let's

get this settled. What did you want to hit me for? If you think I'm after your job on the team, you're crazy. You've played a lot more center than I have, and that's the position you like. I don't. I'd rather be a forward any time. All I came out for was to try to

help while Johnson's hurt. And I'll play anywhere Brent thinks he can use me."

Joe had no answer. His eyes dropped but his jaw was still set stubbornly. "Okay," he said, "have it your way. But I'm puttin' up a scrap for the job." And he left them abruptly.

*　*　*

They played Morton on Tuesday night of the following week in the home gym. Fortunately the Morton squad was young and inexperienced, for Clem Johnson's injury had left a big hole in the Hackersville attack. They missed his smooth rebounding under the basket.

Peewee hadn't practiced but he was allowed to dress for the game, and he sat on the bench through the first three quarters. By that time the Hornets had a good lead. Against a weak defense the boys were shooting well. The coach used Pulaski and Sedgely alternately in the center post and there wasn't much to choose between them.

With a twelve-point margin and only three minutes to play, Brent looked around at his second-stringers.

"Jones—Cooley—Hoskins," he said, "get warmed up."

"Gee, Coach," Peewee pleaded. "How about me?"

But Brent shook his head. "I'm saving you for the tough ones," he said. "This game's in the bag. You'll be able to practice tomorrow and maybe you'll get in against Clay City Thursday night."

Clem Johnson was sitting beside the little redhead. He patted Peewee on the knee. "Take it easy, boy," he grinned. "You an' me got to get well quick as we can. Best way is not to fret."

They won that one by a 41-32 score, and the towns-people of Hackersville picked up heart. Three wins against one loss wasn't a bad record. Perhaps this team was going somewhere after all.

With only forty-eight hours between games, Wednes-day's practice was an important one. The doctor said Johnson's leg was coming along nicely, but Brent decided to go on with his makeshift line-up. He wanted his big key man fully recovered before he let him play again. With Peewee back on the floor they had two full teams dressed, and the second string gave the varsity a real scrap.

The little forward found he had plenty of wind, in spite of his lay-off. Delivering papers every morning had given him the exercise he needed. But his shoot-ing was off at first. It wasn't until the last few minutes that he recovered his accuracy. Right at the end of the practice he pulled off a neat lay-up on a fast break, and followed it a moment later with a long, difficult set shot.

Clay City was one of the teams that had beaten the Hornets the year before. They had lost some star players by graduation, but a big squad had enabled them to fill the gaps, and they were riding a two-game winning streak when they came to the Hackersville gym that Thursday night.

Every bench along the sides of the floor was filled with spectators and an overflow crowd jammed the running track above. The Hornets' girl cheer-leaders, in their green sweaters and white skirts, pranced and cavorted in front of the rooting section, whipping up excitement.

Peewee had never paid much attention to girls. Still, he thought one of the yell-leaders looked pretty cute in her green and white outfit. She was small, like himself, but full of ginger, and a mop of short blonde curls framed her eager face. He knew her casually from freshman English class. Her name was Dotty Gordon.

He didn't have many opportunities to glance her way, for the squad was whirling under the basket, taking warm-up shots. Thornton's suit had arrived the day before, and his bandages were gone. He blended into the team and looked like one of them now.

When the game began he came and sat beside Peewee on the bench, for Pulaski was starting at center. The smaller boy looked up at him curiously.

"I heard," he said, "that you were headed for Brampton Prep. I'm glad you didn't go."

Thornton stared straight ahead. "That was before—

before the accident," he answered. "I doubt if we could afford it now. And anyhow, I'd rather be here."

The Hornets got off to a ragged start. They fouled up several plays and when they scored their first point, on a penalty, Clay City had a 6-1 lead.

Brent called a time-out and laid down the law. "Your teamwork's off," he said. "Never mind the shooting. You'll get your eyes back. But if you don't concentrate on your timing and passing you'll have mighty few chances to shoot. Get out there and make those plays click."

Their floor work began to improve after that. Johnny Gale got the pattern moving and the field goals followed. At the quarter they had pulled up till they trailed by only two points, 11-9. That was as close as they could get for the rest of the first half. The coach sent Sedgely in for Pulaski after the intermission, and he made a nice pivot shot to tie it up.

From then on it continued to be a nip-and-tuck game. First one team went a point or two ahead, then the other caught up. Brent fidgeted on the bench, his face grim.

"They're onto our plays," Peewee heard him mutter. "Got us bottled up."

Clay City was leading, 39 to 38, at that point, and they were well into the final period. Jerry Donovan, with four personals against him, was playing a cautious game, taking few chances. And Gale, Marchetti and Greenbaum seemed to have lost their touch.

Brent swung around suddenly to the small redhead on the bench. "Get your sweat suit off and warm up," he barked.

Peewee needed no second invitation. He whipped off his jacket and pants and started trotting up and down. Somebody in the stands gave him a yell of encouragement. Then the Clay City center fouled Gino under the basket, and as the whistle blew, the coach sent Peewee in to replace Donovan.

He got into position in time to watch Marchetti sink his foul shot. Then, with the score tied, they were racing down the floor to block the attack. In spite of Johnny Gale's close guarding one of the Clay City forwards got off a shot. It hung on the rim of the basket, then rolled off without going through. Their tall center grabbed it in midair and laid it up again—then still again, in a succession of frantic rebounds. The third time Thornton jumped high and batted the ball out to a corner, where Ben Greenbaum recovered.

Practically the whole Clay City team swarmed around him, but Ben sidestepped them coolly, bounce-passing to Marchetti who started on a fast break down the floor. Just after he crossed the center line a whistle blew.

"Running with the ball!" called the referee.

A howl of protest rose from the Hornet rooters, but

it did no good. Clay City took the ball out and launched a fresh attack. Once more they peppered the basket with shots, and once more luck was with the Hornets. This time Thornton caught a rebound in both hands and heaved a long pass to Peewee. He and Gino had hung back, hoping for just such a development. Now they sprinted for their target with only a single opposing guard to block their way. It was a perfect "two-on-one" play. As the guard made a lunge at the little redhead he flipped the ball to Marchetti and Gino split the cords. Ten seconds later the game was over.

CHAPTER 8

WHEN THE WEEKLY *Clarion* came out, next morning, the Hornets were on the front page once more. Their four wins against one loss looked like news to the editor and he made the most of it. Many of those who had attended the game were less impressed. Mr. Carson was one of them.

"There's something wrong with this team," he told Peewee at dinner. "The way they played most of the game, they deserved to lose. As it was, I guess you were pretty lucky."

Peewee admitted the luck, but he had more confidence than his father. "Wait till we get Clem Johnson back in there," he said. "I bet he'd have made a ten-point difference last night. Joe tries hard but he hasn't got that smooth touch. Thornton was a little better. He isn't used to our plays yet, though, and he's never played center very often. Just wait till next week."

Mr. Carson laughed. "Sure," he said, "you'll probably trim Ringsboro without much trouble. They haven't won a game yet, have they? But it'll be a different story when you go down to the city to play Franklin Tech, Thursday night."

Peewee didn't reply to that. He knew most of the squad felt nervous about meeting last year's metropolitan champs. He had seen Franklin play and his own private opinion was that the Hornets could give them a tough game if they were at their best.

How Hackersville had been able to get on Franklin Tech's schedule was a mystery to some of the townspeople. Most of the city high school teams played only teams in their own league. However, the big technical school had had an open January date and offered it to the Hornets. Brent chuckled when he heard about it. "They needed an easy one—a breather—before their game with Central," he had told Speck Newbury. "I guess they looked around for somebody they were sure they could beat, and we're it."

There was no regular cafeteria at Hackersville High. Nearly all the out-of-town boys and girls brought lunches from home and ate them in an unused classroom that had been fitted up with tables and benches.

In one corner there was a little counter where soup and milk were served.

Peewee had formed the habit of eating there, rather than going home at noon, because most of his friends came from the country districts. Usually he brought a couple of sandwiches and an apple, piecing the meal out with a bowl of soup or a bottle of milk.

Johnny Gale, Clem Johnson, Joe Pulaski and Jim Hoskins all frequented the lunch room. And so, Peewee discovered, did the cute cheer-leader, Dotty Gordon. She liked to have her lunch with the basketball players, and it was a wonder she didn't put on weight, with all the cake and pie and pickles they continually offered her.

Dotty was an easy girl to make friends with. She wasn't a flirt—just on good terms with everybody. And Peewee was glad to be included in the circle.

Not all the noon-hour talk was about basketball. These farm youngsters had their own special interests. Several of them were active in the 4-H Clubs and liked to compare notes on their projects. They talked about pigs and chickens and calves, and about pumps and electric wiring and farm equipment. The girls, Peewee was surprised to find, were just as enthusiastic about 4-H matters as the boys. Some of them went in for raising livestock or dressmaking, but Dotty Gordon had a specialty of her own.

She was, Jim Hoskins privately told Peewee, the

best jelly and preserve maker in the county. At the State Fair the previous fall she had walked off with a blue ribbon and two honorable mentions.

On the Monday after the Clay City game they were gathered around the long table at noon.

"Hey!" Johnny Gale interrupted the general chatter. "That big 4-H party's this week, isn't it?"

"That's right," Jim answered. "Saturday night. There'll be three clubs there—ours and two from the other end o' the county. Dad's fixed it for us to use the Grange Hall."

"What do you do at 4-H parties?" Peewee inquired.

There was a chorus of answers. Good eats, games and square dancing seemed to be most mentioned. It sounded fine.

"How about it, Dot?" Joe Pulaski boomed from the far end of the table. "You goin' to the party with me?"

The little blonde laughed and shook her curly head. "Not this time, Joe," she said. "As a matter of fact, I'd kind of like to go with someone my own size. I thought I'd ask Greg Carson to take me."

Peewee choked on the sandwich he was eating, and had to be pounded on the back. When he finally recovered his breath he still found it hard to answer.

"G-gosh, Dotty," he gasped, "if you really mean that, I'd like to take you—sure!"

"Then you've got a date," she answered promptly.

"I want you to get over being a city slicker and find out how much fun we have in the country."

"You mean," said Jim Hoskins, "if any of us are in shape to have fun after that Franklin Tech game."

"They got you scared?" Joe growled. "Me—I'm lookin' forward to tanglin' with 'em."

When they dressed for practice that afternoon, all eyes were on Clem Johnson. He insisted that the knee had come around satisfactorily and gave him no pain. Some of his shots at the basket showed the effects of his lay-off, but his floor work and rebounding were as good as ever.

"I'm going to do some experimenting in this game with Ringsboro tomorrow night," Elmer Brent told the squad. "I'd like to see if we can get more speed by alternating two sets of forwards. Jerry, you and Gino'll start off as usual. Then I'll give you a rest and put in Peewee and Thornton. That way all four of you ought to stay fresh enough to go at top speed, right up to the end of the game."

They tried it out in practice, playing one pair and then the other on the first team. Peewee was happy to find that the edge held by the varsity didn't seem to be lost when he and Sedgely switched over. They sank about as many shots as the regulars. The real margin of superiority was in the smooth teamwork of Johnny Gale and Ben Greenbaum, and the way they fed the ball to the pivot man and forwards.

The Ringsboro game was on the home boards, and after the Clay City thriller the Hackersville fans were out in force. By the time the teams came on the floor many people were already standing. The little Hornet band was playing and the girls were leading a cheer when Peewee trotted out with the squad. Dot Gordon bobbed up from a cartwheel as he passed and she flashed him a smile and a wink.

The first quarter went very much as expected. Hackersville pulled out to a long lead in the first five minutes. With the score 12 to 4, Brent sent in his second set of forwards. Eager to do as well, Thornton and Peewee played like whirlwinds. They poured in set shots and lay-ups and it seemed as if they couldn't miss. At the end of the quarter the Hornets were leading 25 to 6.

To their surprise, the coach was frowning. "This isn't close enough to do you any good," he told the boys. "You'll get careless if you don't look out. I'm going to put the second team in right now."

With Jones, Cooley and Hoskins in the line-up, and Sedgely and Pulaski taking turns at center, Peewee found the going harder. Gradually the Ringsboro team began to click. At halftime they had pulled up to trail by only twelve points.

Not until the last few minutes did Brent put in his first-stringers again. Fresh and well rested, they poured in the baskets, and the final score was 52 to 30.

*   *   *

The coach came to call on Jane the next evening. Peewee went into the kitchen to do his homework, but even with the door closed he could hear his father talking in the living room.

"That was a pretty easy game last night," he said. "They didn't give you much competition, did they? But Franklin Tech's going to be something else again. Think you've got a chance?"

"I think so," Elmer Brent answered quietly. "The boys are worried, and I don't mind having them feel that way. I know they'll be on edge and playing their best. You see, nobody realizes yet just how good this team is. I have a hunch they'll rise to the occasion."

There was a moment's silence. Then the coach went on in a low voice, as if he didn't want Peewee to hear. "I found out one important thing in the Ringsboro game," he said. "We've got two sets of forwards that are just about equal. That boy of yours, small as he is, can really play basketball. So can young Sedgely. Of course, we don't have the same kind of depth in the guard positions. But if anything happens to Johnny or Ben I can shift Gino Marchetti back to a guard spot and still have a strong five on the floor."

When the squad took the afternoon train to the city next day, there was a cheering crowd at the depot to see them off. The band, the yell-leaders and some of the students and parents would be driving down later by car. Brent wanted his team to arrive early and get some rest before game time. With money supplied by the Rotary Club he steered the boys to a downtown hotel and took two rooms where they could relax. Thornton Sedgely disappeared soon after they arrived. He didn't say where he was going but Peewee thought he knew.

The coach supervised their early supper at 5:30, making sure none of them ate too much. Then he made a phone call. When he came back he was grinning.

"We're not going to be playing in the Franklin gym," he told the boys. "The game's been switched to the Field House at the University. It's a big place—a lot bigger than you've ever played in—but the floor's regulation size. You won't have to run any farther or shoot any higher than you do in Hackersville. And remember, Franklin won't feel much more at home than you do. That's a break for our side."

"Gosh!" said Johnny Gale. "The Field House! Isn't that where they play the state high school championships?"

Brent nodded. "That's right," he said. "Better get used to it."

The boys who heard him stole glances at each other. Was it possible, Peewee wondered, that the coach had meant his remark just the way it sounded? They didn't find out then, for there was a knock at the door and several of their fathers came barging in.

"Hear the game's out at the University," said Mr. Carson. "We've got three or four cars—enough to take you all when you're ready."

Brent looked at his watch. "I guess it's time," he replied. "Get your bags, boys, and stay together when we get downstairs. I don't want to lose any of you. Where's Sedgely?"

Thornton was there in the lobby when they came out of the elevator. There was a tenseness about his face, Peewee thought, and when he looked closely he could see that the other boy's eyes were red. They got into the Carsons' Buick together.

"I suppose you went to the hospital," said Peewee softly.

Thornton nodded but it was a moment before he answered. "I saw them both," he said. "Mother and Dad. He—he looks awful, but he's so darn game! Told me to forget all about him and go out and beat those big-town kids! He'll be pulling for us, too. The game's going to be broadcast, and he begged until they let him have a radio in his room."

The boy choked up at that point, and Peewee knew better than to ask him any more questions.

It was only twenty minutes past seven when the car rolled through the wide campus gates and up a drive flanked by overhanging elms. Lights blazed in the dormitories and fraternity houses. Along the snowy walks moved groups of students, heading toward the library. Occasionally they heard snatches of song. At that hour there were only a few cars in the parking space next to the Field House and they left the car there.

A building attendant let them in and led the way through a long, echoing cavern underneath the stands. At intervals they could look up the ramps into the vast, shadowy arena.

"Man, oh, man!" murmured Gino Marchetti under his breath. "It looks bigger'n the Yankee Stadium in there!"

The visiting team's dressing room to which they

were taken was likewise a big place—clean and comfortable, with benches, lockers, showers and stacks of fluffy white towels. Subdued by the size and magnificence of it all, the boys changed their clothes in silence. Finally Johnny Gale laughed.

"Come on, gang!" he said. "What is this—a wake? We're here to play a basketball game. Remember? An' we're goin' to make it a good one. Talk it up!"

They grinned and tried a few feeble wisecracks, but Peewee could see they were still scared.

"You know I've played here a couple o' times," he remarked casually. "That was in the Midget League finals, so I'm not bragging. We won't have too big a crowd tonight, an' it's really a swell floor—smooth an' fast. The glass backboards may fool you a little at first, but a few minutes o' practice an' you'll get used to 'em."

Their respect for him increased and the tension was broken as they began to ask him eager questions. At 7:40 Elmer Brent came into the locker-room.

"Everybody in uniform?" he asked. "Good. I'm not going to give you any pep talk. Let's go out there now and shoot a few."

CHAPTER **9**

IN SINGLE FILE they made their way up the ramp and
out to the floor. The Field House interior was brightly
lighted now and a fair sprinkling of the eight thousand seats were filled. Over on the opposite side they
could see a little group of Hornet rooters huddled
close together in the stand. The band hadn't yet got
up nerve enough to play, but the green-sweatered
cheer-leaders went valiantly into action as soon as the
team trotted out. A faint, shrill yell came across the
floor to greet them. Weak as it was, it put heart into
the boys.

Elmer Brent passed out an armful of basketballs and
set the squad to work under the hoop. They were
awkward at first. Although most of the stands were

empty, they felt as if the eyes of the whole city were on them. Then, little by little, the green-clad boys began to get the range, peppering the thick plate-glass backboards and dropping clean shots through the cords. They stepped up the pace as their muscles and tongues loosened. "Attaboy, Jerry!" they called. "Nice one, Clem! . . . Hit 'er again, Peewee!"

Under the other basket a big squad in the blue and gold of Franklin Tech was in action. As game time approached, the two officials came out and whistled the teams back to their benches. Franklin's sixty-piece band struck up a fight song, and the Hornets gathered around their coach.

"We'll go in with the regular starting line-up," he said briefly. "I want you to get the jump on 'em if you can. Run their legs off in the first five minutes. This is one where I figure surprise will pay off."

From right behind them came a thin but stout-hearted yell. "Yea, Hornets! Bz-z-z! Bz-z-z! Bz-z-z!" They bent in their huddle for a moment, heads close together and hands clasped. Then the varsity five went out to take their positions. In that nervous moment while they waited for the toss-up, Peewee had his first good look at the Franklin five. They were all tall, rangy lads, and they had a bean-pole center by the name of Lukatz who towered over Clem Johnson by a good four inches. They were grinning and re-laxed as they looked down on their smaller opponents. It was fairly obvious that they didn't expect much of a tussle from this little hick-town outfit.

When the whistle sounded, Clem was a shade too eager on the jump. He touched the ball but the lanky Franklin player deflected it to one of his guards, and they brought it down floor in a series of leisurely passes. The center moved into the pivot and went up for what looked like an easy lay-up. It missed, and on the rebound Clem jumped high to recover the ball. His pass out to Johnny Gale was long and true. The Hornet captain dribbled fast down the sideline and tossed overhand to Gino in the far corner. Before the defense caught up with him he swished a two-pointer through the hoop.

That was only the start. Ten seconds later Jerry Donovan stole the ball from a bewildered guard and made a solo dash for the basket, winding up with another score. The big-town team didn't like it. They charged down like a herd of stampeding buffalo. A husky forward blundered into Ben Greenbaum and drew a penalty. With the game barely a minute old, the Hornets had five points.

They not only held that lead but steadily increased it as the first quarter progressed. When Marchetti got away on a fast break and caged a one-hand shot to make the score 13-5, the Franklin coach called for a time out. Breathing hard and sweating but happy, the green-shirted team came back to their bench.

Elmer Brent tried not to show how pleased he was. "You've done what I told you, all right," he said. "But you missed a couple you should have made, and some of your passing looked ragged. They're upset now but they won't stay that way. Remember, this bunch has been winning games against tough competition. So look out for 'em now."

He turned to Clem Johnson. "Leg holding up?" he asked, and the center nodded.

"You and Ben and Johnny'll have to stay in," Brent continued. "So you'd better slow down a bit. I'm putting in Thornton and Peewee and you can let them do the hustling for a while."

The second-string forwards reported at the scorer's table and time was in again. Franklin had also made substitutions in the line-up. Peewee found he was facing a lean, quick-moving Italian boy, only an inch or two taller than himself. The other Franklin guard tossed the ball in to start play and Peewee had to pour on full speed to keep up with his opponent.

For the next few hectic minutes he was in the middle of a whirlwind. Something had happened to the Tech team. They dodged and feinted and passed the Hornets dizzy. Luckily for Hackersville most of the Franklin shots went wild, but Peewee knew his team was being outplayed on the floor. At the end of the quarter, with the score 14 to 9, he was glad to pause and recover his wind.

Thornton grinned at him. "Trying to make it tough for us, aren't they?" he panted. "That kid you're playing is a real whiz but you've been staying right with him."

The Hornets had possession as the second period got under way, and Johnny Gale deliberately slowed down the pace. He and Ben held onto the ball, passing cannily till the pattern formed. Twice they got it in to Johnson, in the slot, but Lukatz was all over him and he had to get rid of it.

Ben Greenbaum gave Peewee a wink as they passed each other in the weave. The little redhead edged outside. His guard followed at his heels suspiciously, then spun away as the ball went to Clem once more. The center faked a shot, but once more he was covered. He pretended to pass toward Johnny, then rifled the ball out to Peewee. Ben had slipped across to screen for him and the little forward had time to get set. His thirty-footer brushed the glass, bounced gently on the back rim and fell neatly through.

Brent left his replacements in for the rest of the half. Sometimes Peewee wondered why, for a hopped-up blue and gold team was giving them all they could handle. Occasionally the Hornets were able to control the ball, giving themselves a chance to catch their breath, but most of the time it was a furious race up and down the floor. The shooting on both sides improved. Twice Thornton Sedgely scored with those graceful California jump shots of his. Clem Johnson put in a pair from the pivot, and Johnny Gale fired a long one from mid-floor that went through. Peewee, fouled in the act of shooting, caged both his penalty tries.

But Franklin was matching them, basket for basket, and scoring an extra goal or two for good measure. At the end of the first half they had pulled up within four points—28 to 24.

Back in the dressing room during the intermission, Elmer Brent took his coat off and worked like a beaver. He massaged the legs of the three men who had to play full time, pointed out mistakes that had been made and gave them a few words of encouragement.

"The team that's behind at the half," he said, "has one advantage over the one that's in front. When they look at that scoreboard they can see just what they've got to do to catch up, so they try all the harder. Here's what I want you to do. Go out for this second half and act as if *you're* trailing. Because you will be, quick enough, if you ease up. Fight for those baskets. Hang onto the ball. And when you get a chance to shoot, make your shots count. Jerry and Gino, you're going in again. It won't be as easy this time, but see if you can get the jump on 'em the way you did at the start."

The squad warmed up briefly under the basket and

came back to the bench at the warning whistle. A moment later the third period began.

Like Hackersville, the Tech team had gone back to its original line-up, but there was a difference now. No longer cocksure of victory, the boys looked grim and determined as they faced off on the court. The Hornets got the ball on the jump, but the defense ran with them stride for stride on the sprint for the basket. They had to maneuver for a while before they got a shot. Finally Gino feinted the tall center out of his way and popped one in from close quarters.

Franklin retaliated quickly. A lucky long shot rolled around the rim and toppled in. Jerry Donovan, fighting aggressively to get the ball, was caught fouling on the same play, and the penalty conversion narrowed the margin to a skimpy three points.

Goals were harder to get after that. Both teams were guarding closely, holding down possible shots. The one advantage the Hornets had was off the backboard. Clem Johnson was outjumping his rival and pulling down the rebounds. When the third period ended, the score was 37 to 34, with Hackersville still ahead.

The Tech coach sent out fresh substitutes to start the final quarter, but Brent kept his first string in.

"Jerry's got four personals against him," he told Peewee. "If he fouls out we'll make a switch."

They could see that Jerry was doing his best to steer

clear of trouble. Once he pulled back when he should have battled for the ball, and the speedy little Italian guard slipped past him to score. As the minutes passed, however, the Hornets succeeded in hanging onto their slim lead. The scoreboard read 41-38 when a whistle halted the play.

"Charging," barked the referee. "Number three!" And dejectedly Jerry Donovan put up his hand.

"That does it," said Brent. "You're in, Thornton and Peewee. Ben looks tired and he's limping, so Gino'll have to take over for him. Go get 'em!"

*　　*　　*

A pale, gaunt-faced man lay in a private room at St. Francis Hospital. The shaded lamp on the bedside table showed his eyes closed. One of his thin hands held tight to the fingers of the pretty woman who sat quietly beside the bed. And from a radio in one corner of the room an excited male voice rattled steadily on.

"This is a thriller, folks," it was saying. "A much better game than we'd been expecting. Here come a couple of substitutions for Hackersville. Let's see— number eleven and number ten—that's Sedgely and Carson. They did all right when they were in before. Sedgely's scored eight points and Carson seven. That little Carson's something to watch—about as big as a peanut, but can he move!

"All right, there's the throw-in. The score's 41 to

39 now, you know, so anything can happen. Gale takes it down—pass to Marchetti—to Johnson—back to Carson—oh, oh! Little Buffo grabbed it in the air! He's off like a streak—only Carson with him—Carson's got his hands on the ball. They're wrestling for it—both of 'em on the floor. There's the whistle and there'll be a jump. This ought to be good, folks—the two smallest men on the court. Up they go—wow! Buffo tapped to Bailey and he's trying a push shot. No good. Johnson gets the rebound. Watch this! Sedgely's all alone down floor. A lo-o-ong pass! He's got it—he's under—it's in! Hackersville takes a four-point lead with less than three minutes to go."

The man on the bed smiled a little and his grip tightened on his wife's hand.

"Don't give up, you Franklin fans," the sports an-

nouncer continued. "Plenty of time yet. And here they come! You can hear 'em pounding down the floor. Lukatz in the pivot—nice pass from Bailey—he spins and lays it up—it's good! That makes it 43 to 41, in a real spine-tingler.

"The clock says two minutes to go. What'll this little team from up-state do now? Freeze the ball? It looks that way. But they're having trouble. The Tech boys are pressing. Eight seconds—nine seconds—they finally got it over the center line just in time. Yes, folks, it's a freeze all right. Look out, now! Lukatz tangles with Johnson, both grappling for the ball. Could be a foul. No—it's ruled a jump ball. This is what you'd call a tense moment. There's the referee tossing it up—they're both in the air—and Lukatz tips it! Bailey to Buffo—to Craig—to Bailey again. He makes a wild stab. It's hanging on the edge—hanging —no! It's in! The score's tied! Listen to that crowd yell!

"Let's see how much time's left—forty-two seconds. This one might go into overtime. Marchetti has the ball out—passes in to Gale and he dribbles down fast. No freeze now. They want a basket. Gale to Sedgely— in to Johnson in the slot—no chance there—he's too well guarded. He fires out to Carson. Looks as if the little fellow meant to try a set shot but Craig and Buffo have him blanketed. Carson gets rid of it on a low bounce to Gale—across to Marchetti—back to Carson. Look out! Sedgely's in the clear! Carson sidesteps Buffo and tosses overhand to Sedgely. Wow! Look at that one-hander! Right through the hoop, and it's Hackersville—the little green team—out in front again! I tell you, folks, whatever happens now, we've seen some great basketball tonight. But remember—it's not over yet by a long shot.

"Here come the big boys from Tech and they've got fire in their eyes! The Hornets are putting on an all-court press—trying to keep Franklin away from that basket. There's some mighty close guarding—they're liable to draw a foul.

"There's Bailey throwing a long pass to Buffo—it's intercepted! Snagged right out of the air by little Carson! He went up for it like a grasshopper—and there he goes! Sedgely's with him—it's two on one—only Craig defending. Carson's going to shoot—no, it's a fake—a beautiful pass over to Sedgely. He lays it up —and it's—good!"

The howl of the crowd drowned out the announcer's voice for a moment. When he could be heard again he sounded hoarse. "That's about it, folks. The gun went off before Franklin could get started again. Too bad, but of course it won't hurt their standing in the city league. Anyhow, there's no disgrace in losing a tight game to a fighting, well-coached team like this one. Our hats are off to the Hackersville Hornets!"

The patient in the hospital bed moved for the first time, passing his left hand wearily across his eyes. "All right, dear," he whispered. "The boy did it. I can sleep now."

CHAPTER 10

IN THE DRESSING ROOM there was a tired but happy bunch of green-jerseyed Hornets. Several excited fathers had joined them while they showered and dressed. Mr. Greenbaum was there, and Mr. Jones and Peewee's own dad.

"I guess the city papers'll begin to take notice of you now," Samuel Greenbaum chuckled. "Franklin had a 6-2 won and lost record up to tonight. Where's young Sedgely? I want to shake his hand. Fourteen points, and he was only in there about half the game!"

Thornton was knotting his tie in front of the mirror. He turned around in embarrassment. "It's nice of you to say that," he mumbled. "But the guys who really deserve the credit are Johnny and Ben and Clem and

Gino and Peewee. Anybody can sink shots when they get assists, an' those boys were feeding me all night."

Elmer Brent spoke up. "He's right," said the coach. "It wasn't stars that won this game. It was teamwork. I'm proud of all of you."

There were enough cars to take them all home. Since Brent wanted to sit with Jane in the Carson Buick, Peewee elected to ride in the Gordons' station wagon with Jim Hoskins, Joe Pulaski and the two girl cheerleaders. Thornton Sedgely had gone back to see his mother and would take the late train home.

They had a lot of fun on the two-hour ride. Packed into the two rear seats, they sang songs, kidded each other and giggled at their own funny remarks. Only Joe Pulaski found it hard to join in the hilarity. Peewee knew the big lad resented the fact that he had had no share in the victory, and he felt genuinely sorry for him.

The station wagon drove through Hackersville to take Peewee home. As he started to get out Dot Gordon squeezed his hand. "Don't forget Saturday night," she said. "See you at my house about half past seven."

Peewee worked hard to make himself presentable for the party. He took a bath before supper and spent half an hour shining his shoes, slicking his hair and picking out his most becoming tie. Naturally he took some ribbing from Jane when he came downstairs.

"Goodness!" she exclaimed. "Don't we look nice? I

bet those farm girls will really swoon when you walk in, small fry!"

"Stop it, Jane," her mother scolded. "You ought to be glad to have him dress up—always fretting about how sloppy he looks. Besides, I'm happy he's taking an interest in girls."

Red-faced, Peewee made his escape. It was a fine night, not too cold, and fortunately the roads were clear of snow so that he could ride his bicycle.

The Gordon farm was only two miles from town, and he arrived punctually at seven-thirty. Dotty's mother came to the door. She was an attractive woman, small and vivacious like her daughter. She welcomed him into a big, comfortably furnished living room and chatted with him while they waited for Dotty to come down.

"I didn't get to the game," she said, "but I was listening to it on the radio, and I read the account in yesterday's paper. Dorothy says you played wonderfully. This team's getting to be famous, isn't it?"

"Mr. Brent's a good coach," Peewee replied. "And he's lucky to have boys who've played together—Johnny and Clem and Ben and Jerry and Gino. But on top of that he's got Thornton Sedgely, and I think he's as good as any of them. If we can keep from getting hurt, we might even get into the state tournament this year."

She smiled. "That's in March, isn't it? My, wouldn't that be fine! I'll be keeping my fingers crossed for you."

Peewee heard light steps on the stairs and got to his feet. Dotty wore a tan sweater and a green skirt, and with her bright curls fluffed out she looked like a dandelion.

"Hi, Greg!" she cried. "All set? You're looking mighty ready. Let's go take the party by storm!"

The Grange Hall was at a crossroads only a quarter of a mile away and the two youngsters found it a pleasant walk. Neither of them had much to say on the way, but it was a comfortable kind of silence. Finally Dotty broke it.

"I hope you're going to like this gang," she said. "They're all good kids. You don't mind my introducing you as Greg, do you? Peewee sounds a little silly. Besides, you'll lose it when you grow up. My brother was about your size till he was fifteen, and all of a sudden he began to shoot up. He's at the university now, and he's six feet tall!"

"Gosh," said Peewee fervently. "I hope that happens to me. My dad's tall enough, and so's Mother. No, I don't care what you call me, but I do like Greg a little better."

The Grange Hall was upstairs, over a general store. The lights were on when they got there, and they could hear voices and laughter. A dozen boys and girls of high-school age were already there, and more arrived every few minutes. Before eight o'clock a crowd of about forty had assembled.

They made Peewee feel at home from the start. The games they played were lively, old-fashioned ones like spin-the-platter and musical chairs. Then, when they were well warmed up, Joe Pulaski brought out his fiddle and Jim Hoskins produced a harmonica.

"Choose your partners and form your sets!" Johnny Gale shouted.

Dot grabbed Peewee's arm. "Come on," she laughed. "Let's get into a good set."

They joined three other couples in the middle of the floor and took their place in a circle. "If you've never done any square dancing," said Dot, "you'll find it isn't much to learn. Here—I'll show you how to do a 'dosey-do'—and I can steer you through the rest of it."

The boys struck up a lively version of *Skip to my Lou,* and Peewee found himself swinging to the rhythmic step with the others. Before the first figure was over he had the hang of it and was enjoying himself thoroughly. A comical, long-legged boy from one of the other 4-H clubs called the figures in a drawling sing-song. After two or three dances he took over the fiddle from Joe Pulaski, and when Joe cut in with Dotty, Peewee had to find another partner. He looked around hastily for a girl his own size, but before he could spot one Clem Johnson appeared beside him.

"This here's my sister Luella," the tall boy said with a grin. "If you want to dance, she'll show you some fancy steppin'."

Luella was a big, jolly girl, nearly as tall as her brother, and Peewee felt a little foolish as he moved into a set at her side. In a moment, however, his shyness was forgotten. She was graceful and light on her feet, and she guided him through an intricate number in perfect time to the music.

"Clem's told me about you," Luella told him as they promenaded back to their corner. "He says you're the smartest little player the Hornets have had in a long time."

"Gosh!" he said in confusion. "I only wish it was true, but coming from a guy as good as your brother, that's some compliment!"

There were other sets and other partners. A little before ten some of the girls went back to the kitchen at the rear of the hall. Peewee had been dancing with Dotty and was sorry to see their set broken up. But a few minutes later he felt better about it.

The boys put up long trestle tables and food began to appear—piping-hot creamed chicken in patty shells —platters of buttered rolls—big bowls of potato salad and cole slaw—cups of steaming cocoa.

"Don't eat too much, now, Greg," Dotty warned him as they sat down. "You've got to save room for some of my pecan chocolate cake. I made the jam, too. It's raspberry. Here—try some on a roll."

It was a feast he wouldn't soon forget. The farm boys' appetites matched the girls' good cooking and everybody got up from the table in a happy mood. The party broke up shortly after, for the youngsters knew morning chore-time would come all too soon. They said their good-nights, and Peewee walked home with Dotty under the stars.

"You said you wanted to cure me of being a city slicker," he told her. "Well, it worked. I honestly never had so much fun in my life."

She laughed. "I never meant that really, Greg. You're as good a country boy as anybody. Maybe you can even join our 4-H Club some day."

"I wish I could," he answered. "I don't suppose the regular meetings are much like tonight, though."

"Oh, we have fun, but we learn things, too. After the minutes and the treasurer's report we hear talks by different people about their projects. A girl shows how to make nice, flaky piecrust. Or a boy tells just what he fed his hens to get more egg production. Then there are refreshments and maybe we have a charade or something. You know, Greg, we've got one or two town boys in the club. If you're really interested, and we can think up a good project—think you'd like to join?"

Peewee grinned. "I sure would. Only my main projects right now have to be the paper route and basketball."

As he rode home on his bike that night he felt a warm

glow inside—a sense of really belonging to this friendly countryside and its young people.

*   *   *

Basketball practice went well the next week. Nobody had been seriously hurt in the Franklin Tech game, and although Coach Brent had been afraid they might let down, after being keyed high for a big contest, no such tendency appeared. In fact the boys had gained a new incentive. They worked harder than ever on their plays because they wanted to keep on winning.

To Peewee, one of the most encouraging signs was the way Joe Pulaski was trying. His passing and team play had improved surprisingly, and he was even getting an occasional rebound away from Clem Johnson. As a result, the second team was able to give the varsity a much better workout than it had earlier in the season.

There was a home game with Pikesville that Wednesday night. After the columns of praise that had been showered on the team in the city papers as well as the *Clarion,* the gym was solidly packed with Hackersville supporters. They had come to see a victory and they weren't disappointed.

Pikesville came with a poor record—six defeats against a single win. Its team played a loose kind of game, weak on the attack and uncertain on defense. As a consequence the Hornets had the ball most of the time and poured their shots through almost at will.

At the end of the half, when they had piled up a lead of 31 to 6, Elmer Brent sent in his entire second string and kept them in till the finish. The slaughter continued. Peewee found he could run away from anybody on the opposing team, and his shooting eye was true. In the sixteen minutes he played he made seven field goals and three fouls for seventeen points. The others knew he was on a hot streak and fed him the ball as often as they got it. The final score was a fantastic 63 to 14 and the Hornet fans went home happy.

The sports editor of the Hackersville *Clarion* outdid himself that week. "Our stalwart basketball players," his story ran, "now boast a proud record of seven victories and only one defeat. How many other teams around these parts have done as well?"

Some of the boys were reading this flowery prose in the school lunch room. "If that dope looked at a few out-of-town papers," Johnny Gale snorted, "he'd know the answer to his silly question. Denton hasn't dropped a game yet, an' neither has Allerton!"

"Hey—listen to this!" said Jim Hoskins, snickering as he read over Johnny's shoulder. " 'While all the Hackersville High lads looked like champions in their crushing defeat of Pikesville, special praise must be heaped upon the carrot-colored head of that small but formidable point-a-minute scorer, Gregory (Peewee) Carson. Or perhaps we should say *pint-a-minute* in deference to his diminutive stature.' "

They howled with glee and beat on the table. "Oh, Peewee!" they called. But the boy wasn't there. He had fled outdoors before they got to that embarrassing paragraph.

It took him several days to live it down, but the team's kidding was good-natured and he didn't let it upset him. The nickname of "Pint" hung on for a time, then gradually faded out as people forgot where it had come from.

The Pikesville game had been played the last week in January and it marked the halfway point in their schedule. Eight games lay behind them and eight ahead. The first two contests in February were to be played away from home on Wednesday nights. They were with Windom and Allerton, teams that had always given Hackersville trouble, and with a full week of practice before each one, Brent worked the squad hard.

A convoy of twenty or thirty cars accompanied them to the town of Windom, over in the next county. Perhaps the team, like the townspeople, were a little over-confident. At any rate, the Windom five put up a surprisingly tough battle, and led by two points at half-time.

Elmer Brent walked up and down in the dressing room. "Don't kid yourselves," he told them. "It takes fight to come from behind, and you don't look like tigers to me—not so far. Maybe you've been reading your press-clippings. You won't enjoy 'em so much to-morrow if you drop this one."

His scorn got under their hides. In the first few minutes of the second half the varsity team tossed in five consecutive field goals. Peewee and Thornton, restless on the bench, were put in at that point, and there was no break in the Hornets' scoring streak. The California boy hit on a beautiful jump shot, Clem Johnson tipped one in from the pivot and Peewee connected with a high-arching set shot that traveled thirty feet.

Windom called a time-out and did better when they returned to the floor, but they never recovered the lost ground. The final score was 45 to 38 in Hackersville's favor.

The green team's backers drove home jubilant after that victory, but when they read the papers next morning there was news that sobered them. The next game, scheduled for February 10th, was to be played on the home court of the Allerton Tigers. Allerton was an industrial city of 40,000 and its high school always had good teams. Twice in the last five years they had captured the state championship. And on the same night that Hackersville had beaten Windom the Tigers had played Denton in the Denton gym.

"Allerton pushes undefeated string to eleven," read the headlines. "Tigers swamp Denton by 52-35 score."

Mr. Carson showed it to Peewee at breakfast after the boy had brought home the paper. "Looks as if you were headed for trouble," he said. "Denton trimmed the Hornets and look what Allerton did to them!"

Peewee nodded. "I guess they're mighty good," he agreed. "But don't give up, Dad. They haven't beaten us yet."

CHAPTER 11

THEY HAD A WEEK to get ready. Elmer Brent knew he had to get the team up for Allerton if they were to have a chance, and he made them work.

"They've got a big, rugged squad down there," he told the boys at their first practice. "They won't be as rough as Red Creek, but they'll crowd you all the way. You can't afford to make mistakes against a team like that, because if they get that ball away from you they've got plenty of scoring punch. That's why we're going to concentrate on fundamentals—good, fast passing and smart faking—yes, and tight defense. If you look as if you're ready we'll work on some new plays, too."

He gave special attention to Jerry and Peewee that week. "You boys are both fast," he told them, "and you've got natural body balance and footwork—things a lot of players never learn. But if you're going to outwit those big guards you need to polish up your deception. Let's try some feints."

Giving Jerry the ball he set himself in defensive position, legs bent a little for spring, arms spread to block a shot or a pass. The Irish boy took a quick step to the left, then attempted to dart around him to the right, but the coach moved with him. Again Jerry tried it and again he was foiled.

"That was a pretty good foot fake," Brent told him. "It didn't work because I was watching your eyes. Now you guard me and I'll show you a trick."

Jerry set himself pugnaciously, arms flailing like a windmill. The coach feinted to his right, then looked up at the basket rim and lifted his shoulders a little. Instinctively Jerry went up on his toes and reached high to deflect the shot. At that instant Brent drove to the left, bouncing the ball out in front of him in a fast dribble. And a second later he laid it up for a goal.

"See what I mean?" he asked with a grin. "You thought I was shooting. Why? Because I looked at the basket and hunched my shoulders. But I kept the ball low and still had my feet in position to cut around. The eye fake is better than the foot fake every time. It gave me a chance to make my move while you were still up in the air. Try it a couple of times and let's see how it works."

When Jerry had practiced the play once or twice, Brent called Ben Greenbaum over. He was generally considered the best defensive man on the squad.

"Come here and put a press on this guy, Ben," said the coach. "He's got the ball. Don't let him get rid of it."

The guard moved into tight defense position and Jerry bounced the ball once. He feinted left, feinted right, looked up at the basket and lifted his shoulders. Ben's reaction was automatic. As he went up for the block, Jerry ducked and darted under his lifted arm. Like a flash he jumped and sank a two-hander through the hoop.

Peewee tried it next. After watching Jerry's success he caught on quickly, and even after the regular guards knew what was coming, he was able to break away twice out of three times. Then, when he had them expecting the break, he deliberately went through with his set shot.

Jerry and Peewee both used what they had learned in team practice that day. There weren't too many opportunities for eye faking, but when the chance arose they made the most of it. As far as Jerry was concerned, that was the end of the lesson. Peewee was different. He got to thinking about all kinds of basketball plays that night and lay awake for an hour imagining ways to fool his opponents. When he finally fell asleep he still dreamed of fantastic games in which he scored at will against giant enemies.

They had fine weather most of that week. But the day before the Allerton game the radio weatherman warned of a low-pressure area moving eastward. "Snow will probably start falling in this locality about Wednesday noon," he announced. "It's reaching near-blizzard proportions in some of the states west of us, and we'd better be prepared for several inches at least."

Plenty of Hackersville people wanted to go to the game, but the threat of bad weather discouraged the majority of them. The driver of one of the big yellow school buses volunteered to take the basketball squad and his offer was gratefully accepted. He had room for the eleven players, the little high school band and the cheer-leaders.

They set off on the 50-mile trip merrily enough. Jim Hoskins had his harmonica with him and he accompanied the rest while they sang. The sky had been gray and cold all day. A few spits of dry snow had come in the afternoon but it hadn't begun to fall in earnest until after they started.

About twenty miles from home the driver pulled off the road and stopped. "Got to get the chains on," he told them. "Anybody want to help?"

Most of the boys tumbled out of the bus, laid out the chains on the snowy ground and helped make them fast on the big rear tires. Peewee shivered in the strong wind as he prepared to climb back aboard. The snow was driving past in level streaks, glistening white in the light from the bus windows. In the five minutes they had been standing there it had piled inches deep on the windshield.

Grimly the driver swept it clear with his mitten and shut the door. "Okay," he said, "let's try it again."

The big vehicle rumbled on into the teeth of the storm, its chains clanking in the snow. Jim did his best to cheer them up with lively hill-billy music but the singing was half-hearted now. They could feel the bus laboring as it bucked into deepening drifts.

"What do you think, Peewee?" Thornton Sedgely asked in a low voice. "Won't get there by game time, will we? It's past seven o'clock now."

Peewee stole a look at the speedometer over the driver's shoulder. They were making a bare twenty miles an hour and they still had covered only half the distance. He shook his head.

"Quit worrying, you guys," said Johnny Gale sternly. "Lie back an' take a nap if you can. We'll get there, an' we'll have a ball game, so we might as well be rested an' ready for it."

Coach Brent had gone ahead in his own car, taking Jane Carson with him, and as captain Johnny felt responsible for keeping up the team's morale.

The bus jolted on and they tried to follow his advice.

Peewee saw an empty seat across the aisle and moved over to it. He curled up, closed his eyes and did his best to forget the howl of the wind and the rattle of sleet outside. After a while he must have gone to sleep, for he had no idea how much time had passed when the bus lurched to a jarring stop.

The wiper blades worked squeakily back and forth across the windshield, and through the arcs they made Peewee could see the headlights boring into a solid curtain of whirling white. The driver muttered something and pushed the gearshift lever into reverse. He backed a few feet, then went into low and plowed into the drift again. It was no good. The bus shook and the engine stalled.

Somewhere toward the rear a girl began to sob. Peewee looked back and saw it was one of the cheer-leaders.

Dotty Gordon had her arm around the frightened youngster and was trying to comfort her.

"Well," said the driver, getting to his feet, "looks like we're stuck. Maybe you won't get to the game but you won't freeze to death, either. I got plenty o' gas in the tank."

He started the engine again and let it idle.

"Wonder if the rest o' the cars got through," Ben Greenbaum speculated. "They were mostly ahead of us, an' I haven't seen anything on the road for half an hour."

Nobody had an answer and the squad settled back into a glum silence. It was five minutes later that they heard a deep rumble in the distance. Peewee and several others jammed into the front end, staring out into the night. The rumble grew louder, and they could begin to see a glow of light through the snow.

"Could be a plow," the driver said. "Just have to wait an' see."

The minutes dragged by but the light kept coming slowly nearer. At last they could see the outline of a tall machine and a great plume of snow flying to the opposite side of the road.

"Motor grader," said the driver. "Got a V-plow an' blower. We'll be out o' here pretty quick."

The big plow roared up abreast of them and halted. "Hey!" yelled the man in the cab of the grader. "You got a shovel?"

The bus driver rolled down his window. "No," he shouted back. "Can you lend us one?"

"Sure, come an' get it."

Several of the boys piled out and floundered through the drift toward the grader. In a moment they were back with a broad-bladed snow shovel. It took them only a few minutes to clear a path to the left, connecting with the plowed half of the road. Then Gino ran back to return the shovel while the bus driver revved up his engine. He had to rock back and forward once or twice to get traction, but by the time the boys were inside he had pulled out on the road behind the plow.

It was nearly nine o'clock when they rolled into the city and drew up in front of the high school. There were lights in the big gymnasium, and in spite of the storm a fair-sized crowd was waiting impatiently for something to happen. The Allerton coach met the visitors at the dressing-room door.

"Brent called up," he told them. "He's marooned at a farmhouse, somewhere up the road, so you'll have to go ahead and play without him. He said your captain was to take charge. By the way, is one of you named Carson?"

"That's me," said Peewee.

"Brent wanted me to tell you your sister's all right. He'll bring her home tomorrow, soon as the roads are cleared."

The boy's face was red and the coach grinned as he showed them where to dress.

They got into their uniforms as fast as they could. The crowd greeted their arrival on the floor with hoots and stampings and it was a flustered squad that began pitching practice shots at the basket.

"You'll have to cut that short," the referee told them. "It's an hour past starting time now and the home team's been waiting since before eight. I'll give you just three minutes."

After the stiffness that had come from their long bus ride they really needed more time to loosen up, but Johnny Gale didn't like to argue with the officials. When the whistle blew he herded them all back to the bench.

"Well, gang," he said, "I guess it's up to us to do the best we can. The regular line-up goes in, an' we'll just have to do our warming up while we play. Let's work hard from the start. Better not try any tricky stuff till your muscles are loose an' you know you've got the touch."

He gave the names to the scorekeeper and they went out to take their places. All of them except Clem Johnson looked small beside the Allerton team, resplendent in orange and black striped jerseys. The Tigers were big and they were fast. From the opening whistle they were running at top speed. Yet it wasn't "firehouse" basketball they played. They passed smoothly and handled the ball well, waiting for the right opening for their shots. Before five minutes had gone by they had hung up five field goals and led by a 12 to 5 score.

At that point Johnny Gale called for a time-out. He looked grim and worried as he gathered the boys around him. There was no question about their being warmed up now. Every member of the varsity five was panting and wet with sweat.

The captain turned to Peewee. "You've been watching from the bench," he said bluntly. "What are we doing wrong?"

"Nothing I could see," the little forward told him. "It looked to me as if they just got the jump an' kept it. The only way I know to beat that is to get hold o' the ball an' run harder'n they do. With the lead they've got now I'd expect 'em to ease up a little. That'll be your chance."

Gale nodded. "Sounds like sense. But there's one more thing. We've got to tighten up our floor play— keep passing till we've got the basket in our sights an' then really hit. We missed six shots in a row, there at the start. Come on, gang. We're hot an' loose now. Let's go!"

It was the green team's ball out. Ben bounced it in to Johnny who spun a long pass to Clem and they were off. As the defense raced down to cover, Peewee saw Jerry take a quick toss, eye-fake his guard off balance and cut like lightning for the basket. His one-hand jump shot went in, and the little rednead on the bench rubbed his hands and grinned. He wished Brent had been there to see it.

The Tigers roared back but Gino intercepted a high dribble half way up the floor and passed across to Clem. The big center was in the clear, moving like the wind. He leaped for the basket and dropped the ball through. With that start they seemed to catch fire. Allerton connected only once in half a dozen shots, and each time they missed it was Clem Johnson, working beautifully off the backboard, who recovered for the Hornets. Johnny Gale hit from outside, Jerry sank another one, close in, and Gino, fouled as he caught a pass, tied the score with a clean one-pointer. At the quarter it was 14 to 14.

During the brief rest the Hackersville squad discussed ways to keep the pressure on their big opponents. "I hate to switch forwards while we're hot," Johnny Gale explained to Thornton and Peewee. "Let's see how it goes. You'll get your chance later."

Eager as he was to get in, Peewee knew the captain was right. Brent would have made the same decision, he was sure. So he sat back to wait.

The Hornets' streak snapped as abruptly as it had begun. Jerry, trying to break down-floor with a fast dribble, lost the ball on a whistle for traveling.

"Look out—he's sore!" Thornton muttered. And sure enough, a few seconds later, the aggressive Irish boy shoved a shoulder into a Tiger forward in an effort to steal the ball. It was his third personal. The Allerton man missed the first try but laid the second one in, and the big team started to roll again.

Nothing seemed to work for the Hornets after that. They fell behind by three points—five—seven. Gale called another time out with three minutes to go in the half, and put in Thornton and Peewee. Stiff from sitting on the bench, they had trouble getting steam up. Before either of them had really begun to click the Tigers had sunk two more field goals. Just before the whistle the California boy finally connected with a one-hand jump, but the score at half-time stood at 25 to 16 in Allerton's favor.

Johnny Gale looked tired and discouraged as he faced the squad in the dressing room. Wearily he sat down on a bench and stared at the floor without saying anything. He had taken the whole weight of impending defeat on his own shoulders.

"Hey," Gino blurted out, "quit takin' it so hard, Johnny. Sure we've been playin' like dopes, but it's not your fault. Maybe we can come back. Anyhow, we can give it a heck of a try!"

There was a chorus of agreement from all the rest of them. "Sure can!" . . . "We'll stop those big lugs!" . . . "Keep the ball away from 'em an' pepper that basket!"

Johnny's back straightened and he looked up with

an attempt at a grin. "Okay," he said, "I'll quit worrying. What got me down was the sight o' that guy up in
the broadcasting booth telling the world what an easy
game this is for the Tigers. Guess I got to thinking
about the coach, somewhere out in the country, listening to the farmer's radio an' not able to do anything
about it. Let's just remember that, when we get back
on the floor. Come on an' shoot some. This time we
don't have to go in cold."

CHAPTER *12*

IN THE SECOND HALF of that game they threw a scare into the Tigers that the city of Allerton wouldn't forget for a long time. Playing with a kind of desperate fury, the little green team hung onto the ball and fired away at the hoop till they had cut the lead to a bare three points in the last moments of the game. Jerry was out on fouls and Peewee had replaced him.

With less than a minute left, he had the ball twenty feet out. There was no chance for a set shot. The big, muscular guard had him covered too closely. But he remembered Brent's lesson in eye-faking. He shifted his right foot forward to be in position, then looked up at the basket and hunched his shoulders, still holding the ball low. The guard's reaction was automatic.

Up he went on his toes, arms reaching high to block the shot, and Peewee ducked, dribbling to the left like lightning. He almost succeeded in cutting past, but the guard's arm came down in time to catch him on the shoulder and spin him off balance. The whistle shrilled out.

"Foul on Number Seven," called the referee. "Two shots."

Shakily, Peewee moved to the foul line. Under the old rules he could have taken one try and, if he made it, waived the second shot to keep possession in hopes of scoring a field goal. Now he had no alternative. There were still a handful of seconds left. Maybe a miracle might happen.

He took a deep breath to steady himself, bounced the ball and brought it up with his eyes on the hoop. It went through and was passed back to him for the second try. Then, by pure chance, he caught the imploring look in Clem Johnson's eyes. The tall center was in position at the left of the foul lane, nearest to the basket. Peewee thought fast. If he made the point the Hornets would still trail by one and Allerton would have the ball. If he bounced it off the backboard toward Clem without touching the basket he knew it would be declared intentional and again they would lose possession. He had to make it hit the rim.

With all the skill he could summon he tossed the ball upward. For a split second his heart sank. It looked too

good—it was going in. But no! It hung tantalizingly on the left side of the rim and rolled off at last, right into the center's waiting hands. He jumped high and laid it in. The score was tied—44 to 44.

The big timing clock showed fourteen seconds left to play, and the Allerton coach pulled his team off the floor for a huddle before taking the ball in.

On their side of the floor, the Hornets were tired but

happy. "Get that ball!" Johnny Gale urged. "If we go into overtime we're sunk. They've got the power an' the substitutes to outlast us. I reckon it's now or never."

When the ball was tossed in, the green-jerseyed players put on an all-court press. They crowded hard, grabbing at every pass and dribble. In those wild final seconds Johnny Gale and a big Tiger forward bumped shoulders close to the basket. It could have been called either way and some referees might have ignored it. This one didn't. He blasted his whistle and pointed at the Hornet captain.

Johnny had a stricken look as he raised his hand and took his place beside the foul lane to wait for the penalty shots. The first one missed, but the second sailed true to the mark. And before Hackersville could get the ball over mid-court the game ended.

They stumbled back to the dressing room with the exultant cheers of the crowd ringing in their ears. Johnny didn't face the others. He stood with his back to them, fumbling with the door of the locker.

"Well," he said, in a choked kind of voice, "I lost it. You can all blame me."

"Are you nuts?" Ben replied harshly. "Quit talking foolishness. Even if we lost, you did everything anybody could in that game."

The door opened at that moment and a tall man in an overcoat and snowy galoshes strode in. It was Elmer Brent, and he was smiling.

"Sorry I let you down, gang," he said. "I got here as quick as I could. But I heard it all on the car radio, and I'm prouder of you than I've ever been."

*　　*　　*

It was past two o'clock next morning when the last of the bus passengers reached home. The plows had been through all the way but there was some snow still falling and fast driving was impossible. Mrs. Carson came softly to Peewee's door at her usual time, a little after six. She looked in at him, shook her head and smiled as she tiptoed away. The boy groaned and rolled over. Then he threw back the covers. Sleep or no sleep, he had papers to deliver.

When he got downstairs he was surprised to see his father already dressed. "I've got the chains on the car," Mr. Carson told him. "I'll take you around, so you won't have to make two trips on foot."

"Tell me about the game," he said, as they drove along the snowy streets. "The reception was so bad I only got a little of it on the radio."

"Not much to tell," Peewee mumbled. "We got licked by one point. The coach was snowbound an' we played without him. If he'd been there it might've been different."

"Oh, well," his father replied, trying to comfort him, "you can't expect to win 'em all. If you do the best you can that's what counts. Eight and two is still a mighty good record."

They had a Friday night game with Oakmont at home, and this was Thursday. When the squad gathered in the gym after school, Coach Brent looked them over and grinned. "Go on home," he said. "You don't need practice after last night. What you need is sleep. Get rid o' those circles under your eyes and come in here fresh tomorrow."

Peewee went to bed before eight o'clock and slept soundly till six. He felt fine when he went to school, but fatigue and exposure had caught up with some of the other boys. Two of the regulars—Ben Greenbaum and Clem Johnson—were at home with bad colds, and Jerry Donovan had the sniffles.

Elmer Brent studied the situation and rearranged his starting team. He put in Ray Jones at the vacant guard post, and Joe Pulaski and Thornton Sedgely alternated at center. After the first period, when it appeared that Jerry's cold was bothering him, Peewee took over in the forward spot.

The makeshift line-up might have been in trouble if Oakmont had come in with a strong team. As it was, the Hornets played raggedly for sixteen minutes, and only began to pull away in the second half. Then Thornton's smooth rebounding and the solid floor play of Johnny and Gino put the game on ice. Peewee had his shooting eye and they fed him chance after chance. He piled up five field goals and four fouls for a total of fourteen points.

The basketball players were not the only casualties of the storm. Jane Carson missed the Oakmont game. Red-eyed and sneezing she had been put to bed by her mother, and even when Elmer Brent came around on Saturday night to find out how she was, Mrs. Carson refused to let him see her.

"I'm not blaming you," she told the embarrassed young man. "But Jane ought to have more sense than to gallivant around in cars during a blizzard. Right now she looks about as glamorous as something the cat dragged in. You come back next week when she's feeling more like a human being."

Dotty Gordon was also laid up with a cold. After seeing the coach sent away discomfited, Peewee decided not to hike out to the Gordon farm. But the 14th of February was next day, so he mailed her a ten-cent valentine and wrote on it that he hoped she'd get well soon.

On Monday Elmer Brent called together such members of the squad as were available and talked over his strategy for the rest of the season. He had brought a small blackboard to the gym, and on it he charted their games.

"We've played eleven teams so far," he said. "Most of them don't amount to much. Our nine wins and two defeats look good at first glance, but we've only played three really good outfits. Denton was good and we lost. We beat a first-class Franklin team but we dropped that tough one to Allerton. So our average against top competition is only one out of three.

"Now let's take a look ahead. We've got five more games to play, and none of them are against pushovers. Cateston's won better than half of its games so far. Raymond would rather beat us than any other team in the league. We're traditional rivals. And Wilmot's trimmed at least two teams by bigger scores than we did. Those are the 'easy' ones. After that we go down to the city again and tangle with Roosevelt High—one of the best. And our final game's a return engagement with Denton, here at home. Doesn't sound very soft, does it?"

He waited for an answer but they were silent, staring at their feet.

"Hey," he laughed, "don't take it that way. I haven't finished yet. We've got two more days before Cateston comes in here and by that time I expect Clem and Ben'll be back. Jerry's over his cold right now, so we may even have a full squad for the next game. And one game at a time is all we have to think about. If we're going to win this one we need some practice. Let's do it now."

They worked hard for that Cateston game and it was a good thing they did. When Wednesday night arrived Clem Johnson was still laid up with a cold, and

Ben Greenbaum, though he put on a uniform, didn't feel up to par. Brent decided not to let him play. With Gino going back to fill the guard position, Thornton at center and Jerry and Peewee in as forwards, Hackersville presented the smallest line-up of the year. Cateston had no giants but they looked formidable enough alongside the Hornets.

What they lacked in inches the home five had to make up in speed. From the opening jump they ran and passed like demons, and as long as they could keep it up they had an obvious edge on the bigger, slower team. They began scoring in the first minute, when Peewee fed the ball to Jerry for a neat lay-up. Thornton added one from the pivot and Peewee fired a strike from outside. They led by seven points at the quarter and were ahead 21 to 12 at the half.

After the intermission Brent put in Jones for Marchetti at guard and sent Pulaski to the center post, giving Thornton and Jerry a rest. Big Joe's team play was better than Peewee had ever seen it. He not only got his share of rebounds but hit the cords for a goal or two of his own. Meanwhile the little redhead was having himself a night. He played all thirty-two minutes of the game and collected six two-pointers and five foul shots for a total of seventeen of the Hornets' fifty-two points. The final score was 52 to 39 in their favor.

They were proud of that victory but the coach was careful not to let them get overconfident. "Cateston's really better than that," he told them. "Any team can have an off night and we were lucky to catch them when they were down. Generally the luck breaks about even. So don't expect any more easy ones."

He worked them hard the remaining two days of that week. On Monday the invalids were back and in uniform, with a chance for one day's practice before traveling to Raymond. By three-thirty they were out on the floor, eager to start, but at that moment a car drove up to the gymnasium door. The two men who came in said they were looking for Mr. Brent.

While he talked to them, the squad gathered under the basket and took some shots. Their interest was half-hearted, however, for the two strangers claimed most of their attention. One of them carried a Graflex camera and the other was busily writing in a notebook.

"I bet they're from one o' the city newspapers," Ben Greenbaum whispered. "Maybe we'll get a write-up, huh?"

The conference with Brent broke up and the man with the camera strolled over to the players. "Okay, guys," he said, "let's have a group picture first. Line up over here—short men in front, tall ones behind. Closer together. All right, hold it."

The flash bulb popped. "Wait, now," the cameraman ordered. "One more for luck, an' this time look happy. Now let's have some action shots."

He got a picture of Clem Johnson laying the ball in

on a jump, and another of Johnny Gale dribbling down-floor. Then he caught sight of Peewee.

"Hey!" he said. "You play on the team?"

"I'm a sub, mostly," the boy replied.

"Never mind—stand over here beside Johnson, the tall guy. Okay, Johnson—hold out your arm at the side, an' you, little feller, stand under his arm. Okay—smile! That does it. Thanks."

When they were gone Elmer Brent looked anything but pleased. "Newshounds!" he snorted. "Any time a team puts together a fair record they have to do a big build-up for their paper. The kids see their pictures and read how good they are and it goes to their heads. Well—let's forget it. Come on, get out there and do some work for a change!"

He kept them at it fifteen minutes overtime to make up for the interruption but they knew it had been a good practice when they were through.

Tuesday afternoon they packed up their suits, ready to start for Raymond as soon as supper was over. As they left the school building, Peewee saw most of the squad ahead of him, hurrying toward the newsdealer's where the evening paper was on sale. A little ashamed of himself he laid down a nickel and picked up his own copy.

"Here it is!" Jerry Donovan crowed. "Second sport page. Look at that big picture! Gee—my mom'll want to frame this!"

They were all there, in the four-column cut, staring out of the page with stern determination on their faces. The paper hadn't used the smiling shot after all. Below, in a smaller picture, Clem was shown going up for the lay-in. Peewee looked twice to make sure the photograph of himself standing under the big center's arm hadn't been printed. At least, he thought, that was something to be thankful for.

CHAPTER *13*

THE TOWN of Raymond was only fifteen miles away, so they didn't have to rush through supper. For years the Hornets and the Raymond Redwings had been natural rivals. Their high schools were nearly the same size and afforded much the same kind of basketball material. Whichever team won the annual game considered it a successful season regardless of other wins and losses.

This year it was different. Hackersville, sporting a 10-2 record, was being mentioned in the city papers as one of the "hot" teams in the state, while Raymond had so far won only four out of eleven games.

"You'd better be good tonight," Mr. Carson warned as they went out to the car. "From what I hear, those

Redwings are loaded for bear. They'd rather upset you than win the Regionals!"

"I know," Peewee answered. "The coach told us the same thing. We're looking for a tough one."

They found the main street of Raymond plastered with "Beat Hackersville" signs and an overflow crowd milling around the high school gym. Their own cheering section was large, for good weather and civic pride had brought a lot of home-town people to the game. Throughout the warm-up the rival bands played loudly and the cheer-leaders on opposite sides of the floor tried to outdo each other in acrobatics and enthusiasm.

All five regulars went in for the Hornets. Peewee, watching from the bench, could see that they had their hands full right from the start. They weren't loafing and they were shooting well, but this Redwing team was whipped up to fever pitch.

With only half of the first quarter gone and Raymond leading 7 to 6, Brent made a switch at center. Clem Johnson came out, breathing hard and looking tired, and Joe Pulaski went in.

"Sorry, Coach," the tall Negro boy said ruefully. "Guess I haven't got my strength back."

"You're doing fine," said Brent. "I want you to stay fresh because we may need you later."

Big Joe had been itching for this chance and he made the most of it. Almost immediately he wrestled a rebound away from the Raymond center and on the jump-off he tipped to Marchetti. They went down with a fast break and a long pass to Donovan resulted in a score.

The fired-up Redwings came right back with a goal of their own. Throughout the first half the lead continued to change hands, with never more than a two-point spread between the two teams. Raymond held a 23-21 edge at the intermission. Starting the second half Brent sent Peewee in for Donovan and put Sedgely at the pivot spot. "You're behind, boys," he told them. "Time to step on the gas."

They set off with a rush that quickly evened the score. Peewee hit first with a long set shot. Then Thornton put them ahead with a lay-up and Gino stole the ball as their opponents hurried down the floor. His pass went to Thornton in the slot. Peewee faked the defense out of position by cutting fast to the right, and the California boy spun around to drop in a perfect one-hander.

A moment later Johnny Gale captured a rebound off the board. "Easy now," he murmured as he passed to Peewee. "Slow 'em down—they'll go crazy!"

The Hornets went into a tantalizing, controlled offense, playing it safe, passing smoothly. And the Raymond five did just what Johnny had foreseen. Desperate to get the ball they crowded harder and harder till they were almost treading on the attackers' toes. Peewee saw that two men were guarding Thornton.

He got the ball, faked a pass in to the pivot, cut left with a sudden dribble and went up for a close shot. It didn't go in because he was fouled as the ball left his hands.

"Two shots!" barked the referee, and the little redhead stood there and sank them both.

They were never headed after that. In spite of the imploring yells of the home-town crowd, the Redwings' attack petered out. Their timing was off and their shots went wild. With Clem Johnson back at center in the final period the Hackersville boys coasted to a 52-42 victory.

Peewee's father was unusually quiet on the way home. After most of their victories he had had a good deal to say, praising or criticizing the way they had played, making remarks about the officiating.

"I'm beginning to think this team of yours is really good," he said at last, breaking a long silence. "Sometimes I've figured it was luck, but you seem to have the knack of putting out just enough to win, whether the game's hard or easy. I was really scared in that first half. Looked like an upset was cooking. But you came from behind. Even with Johnson out you'd have done all right. Think you could win the Regionals?"

"If we get asked," said Peewee. "Yes, I think we might. The only schools in the Mid-State region with better records are Denton and Allerton. So if they pick four teams for the play-off we ought to be one of 'em."

The state was divided into four sections, or regions, for purposes of settling the basketball championship. They were known as the Northeast, the Northwest, the Mid-State and the Metropolitan, largely made up of city and suburban schools. Regional play-offs were held in the middle of March, after the regular schedules were over. And the four regional champions went on to the All-State Tournament.

The Wilmot game was scheduled for Saturday night of that week. The following Tuesday they were to journey down to the city to play Roosevelt High's Rough Riders, and their final contest with Denton would be played on the home floor—again on a Saturday.

Peewee and his father weren't the only people in town who were thinking about the Regionals. The *Clarion's* sports editor had a big black headline clear across the page. "ONLY THREE TO GO! COME ON, HORNETS!" it screamed. And the story below not only described the victory over Raymond in extravagant prose, but pointed out the team's excellent chance of getting into the play-offs if they could put Wilmot away.

With that incentive in their minds, the boys were eager for work that week. Brent didn't have to urge them. They got to practice early and hated to quit. In the whole picture there was only one thing that worried Peewee. That was the continued coolness between Thornton Sedgely and Joe Pulaski.

It wasn't hard to understand why Joe held his grudge. He was a primitive type of boy, brought up in a rough environment. Proud of his physical strength, it wasn't easy for him to be beaten at anything, and try as he would he could never match the smooth play of the young Californian.

Thornton's attitude was something wholly different. The smiling self-assurance he had shown when he first moved to Hackersville was gone now. He was quiet, co-operative and hard-working as far as school and basketball went. But although Peewee was probably his best friend, the younger boy didn't feel really close to him. Somehow the accident had made Thornton draw into a shell. He hardly ever mentioned his father, yet Peewee was sure he worried about him constantly and brooded over the idea that he himself was to blame for all that had happened.

Liking both boys and wanting harmony on the squad, Peewee had hoped to bring Thornton and Joe together. But the Californian shrugged off his efforts at peacemaking. He simply ignored the big, scowling Pole when they met in the school corridor or the dressing room. On the gym floor their teamwork was good enough but they never spoke to each other.

"Why should I go out of my way to be decent to

that big ape?" Thornton asked. "He offered to sock me once—said the only reason he didn't was that I was hurt. Well, I'm okay now. Let him try it."

Saturday night arrived and Wilmot came to town. They had a scrappy, well-coached team, and a reputation for pulling upsets. On their record they were definitely the underdogs in this contest and they meant to knock off the much-publicized Hornets.

Brent made the situation clear in the locker-room before the game. "This could be the toughest one we've played yet," he told the squad. "And it's the one we've got to win. They probably figure we'll be saving something for the big ones next week. We won't. We're going all out, right from the whistle. But to make 'em think we underrate 'em I'm going to start Joe Pulaski at center, and Thornton and Peewee at forwards. You'll stay in just as long as you're ahead."

Big Joe rubbed his hands. "You hear that, guys?" he chuckled. "Let's make 'em like it!"

It was a smart piece of strategy. As soon as the line-ups were announced, the Wilmot five knew they were facing second-stringers and figured they could pile up a quick lead. Perhaps it made them careless. When Joe got the tap and Peewee darted in for a score in the first ten seconds it threw them off stride. And the eager Hornet subs kept up their furious attack, pouring in goal after goal.

Pulaski was relishing his starting assignment. He was a tiger on rebounds and his passing and shooting from the pivot were effective in spite of his roughness. The one trouble was that he began to collect personal fouls. There were three charged against him when the first period ended. But meanwhile Hackersville had built up a 16 to 7 lead.

"Come on, Coach," Jerry Donovan pleaded. "Give us a chance at those birds!"

Brent grinned and shook his head. "You'll get in," he said, "but not yet. This combination's doing all right."

Wilmot was better organized in the second quarter, but it was too late to do much about it. Between Peewee's speed and faking and Sedgely's hook shots the Hornets held their lead, and with only seconds to go till half-time the score stood 28 to 18 in their favor. That was the moment when Joe Pulaski finally fouled out.

He got a tremendous hand as he left the floor. But the thing that made Peewee happy was to see Thornton run over and slap the big farm boy on the back. In his exuberance he grabbed a pass from Gale, sidestepped his defender and fired at the basket from forty feet out. It dropped through just as the whistle blew.

The first-stringers had been champing at the bit all through the half and when they went in after the intermission they tore into their opponents with pent-up

fury. Brent called time after they had run the score to 38 to 20.

"That's enough crazy basketball for now," he said. "Wild passing and shooting may be fun but it doesn't do your game any good. Slow it down for a while and let's see some real controlled offense."

"Ben an' I—we're all for it," Johnny Gale panted. "We're plenty bushed tryin' to keep up with these eager beavers!"

With Clem Johnson's co-operation the veteran guards steadied the team and held down the pace. They didn't shoot as many baskets but they kept possession of the ball, and the scoring opportunities they gave the frustrated Wilmot five were few and far between. Even when Jones and Hoskins took over the guard posts in the last few minutes, the Hornets held their own. They wound it up with a 50 to 32 score for their twelfth victory.

When Peewee opened the sports section of the Sunday paper next morning, he found a full page devoted to the scoring records of all the high schools in the state. He ran down the column of Mid-State schools. Only Allerton was undefeated in regional play. They had dropped one to Roosevelt in the Metropolitan area and sported a 13-1 over-all record.

Denton, too, had lost only one game, but that was to Allerton. Next came Hackersville with its 12-2 rating. And Clay City, with nine wins against four defeats, stood fourth among the Mid-State teams. Nothing that could happen in the final week of the season seemed likely to change those standings. The Hornets were a sure choice to go to the Regionals.

He walked home from church with Thornton Sedgely that morning and they talked about the team's achievement.

"I bet you never thought," said Peewee, "when you first saw this little country town that you'd have a chance to play on a really hot basketball team. I know I didn't."

Thornton smiled and shook his head. "I've been ashamed a good many times," he said, "when I remember those first days in town. Boy—you must have thought I was a stinker! But after the accident the gang was so swell to me I wanted to crawl in a hole. About the team, though, I wasn't fooled. The first practice I saw I knew they were good. And we're lucky to have a coach like Elmer Brent. He's tops.

"By the way," he added, "you might be interested to hear Joe Pulaski and I have buried the hatchet. I guess we'll never be pals but after last night's game I couldn't hold a grudge against the big lug."

The boy's cheerful mood tempted Peewee to ask him a question.

"What's the word from the city?" he inquired.

This time Thornton really beamed. "Mother called me up before the game, yesterday evening. Dad's out of the woods at last. They'll be coming home this week."

"Gosh!" said Peewee. "That's the best news I've heard in a month o' Sundays!"

CHAPTER 14

THE ROOSEVELT GAME was set for Tuesday night. The city papers that morning called it "a good warm-up contest for the Rough Riders, as they prepare for the Metropolitan play-offs." In spite of their earlier victory over Franklin Tech, the sports writers were still a bit patronizing in speaking of the Hornets.

"The little upstate school from Hackersville," said one columnist, "will bring a very respectable record to match against the Teddies' unbroken string. With a student enrollment of only 96 boys, the Hornets' coach, Elmer Brent, deserves a lot of credit. His players are on the small side and few in number. But they're fast and scrappy, and they should provide the rampaging Roosevelt squad with just the practice they need before their battle for the city championship."

There was no money for train fares or hotels this time, but with twenty or thirty cars making the trip for the game, rides were plentiful. Thornton went with Peewee and his father in the family Buick.

"I hear your dad's coming home," Mr. Carson remarked as they drove down the highway.

"That's right," said the California boy. "He's been up and walking around the last few days. They're taking the train tomorrow."

"The men at the plant'll be mighty pleased to hear that," Mr. Carson told him. "I don't know how many times they've asked about him."

One by one, the members of the squad arrived at Roosevelt's fine stone gymnasium. They had been somewhat overawed on their previous trip to the big town. This time they had more confidence. When they were all assembled, Brent called them together in the visiting team's dressing room.

"They call this a practice game for the Rough Riders," he said. "That's exactly what it is for us, too. Believe it or not, I don't particularly care whether you win or lose. What I want is smooth floor play and careful shooting. According to all the dope, this Roosevelt outfit is terrific. Whether you beat 'em or not, you'll learn plenty from such a team. Everybody understand? All right, finish dressing and let's go."

The coach's words eased their tension. Instead of being tight and nervous as they went through their pre-game practice, they were relaxed and loose, kidding each other.

There was a big crowd in the gym. Three or four thousand basketball fanatics had come out to see the fabulous Teddies win another in their unbeaten march. They laughed heartily at the contrast in size between the two squads, and applauded the efforts of Hackersville's tiny band and cheering section.

At the other end of the floor twenty big youngsters in purple and white were warming up. To Peewee they looked like college men. If any of them were less than six feet tall it wasn't noticeable, and two or three must have stood more than six-feet-six. That didn't bother him, but their shooting did. Every time he looked their way a ball was dropping through the hoop.

The whistle called them back to the bench for final instructions and Brent pulled them close around him. "I've been watching this gang," he said. "They're big and rangy—all arms and legs. They'll block a lot of shots—break up a lot of plays. If they get on you too tight, try bounce-passing. And they ought to be easy to fake against, because most tall kids have slow reflexes. Just don't let 'em run over you. Go ahead, now, and good luck!''

The Teddies' center was even taller and lankier than

Lukatz, of Franklin. He stood half a head above Clem Johnson, who grinned up at him amiably, then out-jumped him on the toss and tipped the ball out to Ben Greenbaum. A quick cross-court pass to Gino, a fake cut-in and a flip to Clem, on the post, wound up in a graceful hook shot that gave the Hornets first blood.

"Yea, Hornets!" shrilled the little group from Hackersville. It looked surprisingly easy, but almost before the yells subsided Roosevelt's giants had gal-loped down the floor, passed once or twice and hung up one of their own.

As Johnny and Ben brought the ball out, one of the Rough Rider guards leaped high to intercept an arching pass. He came down dribbling. Before the defense could form, his solo dash had put the big team two points ahead.

The thing happened so fast it took Peewee's breath away and left him shaky with dismay. He thought surely the Hornets would be thrown off stride. But Johnny and Ben were old hands at the game. They brought it out more carefully this time, bounce-pass-ing, keeping their dribbles close to the floor. Jerry took the ball beyond center court and cut past his de-fender, outspeeding him down the sideline. From the corner he tossed out to Gino, edged in toward the basket and was in position for a lead pass. It reached him safely but his leaping hook shot missed the hoop.

Clem took the rebound and passed out to Ben while Johnny and Gino came over to screen. "The Brain" set himself for his favorite shot. The ball went true to the mark, but just as it arched toward the basket the Roosevelt center stretched up his lanky arm and batted it out to a team-mate.

The Hornet bench groaned. What good were steady team play and fine shooting against a bunch of over-sized freaks like these? But the coach was still smiling and unperturbed. The varsity seemed to be taking it well, too. They hustled down in time to keep the attack off balance, and when the Rough Riders finally tried a shot Clem's magnificent backboard work recovered the ball.

Roosevelt had been working a close pattern so that the whole purple team was pulled in. Of the Hornets, only Jerry had hung back. He took Clem's lightning pass and was off. Long before a defense man could catch him he was under the basket, laying up a clean shot.

That put heart into the Hackersville rooters. They yelled themselves hoarse while the little team continued to battle valiantly. Peewee could hear Ben and Gino talking it up, shouting words of encouragement to the others. Then, as the pace stepped up, they were silent, saving their breath for running.

At the start it had looked like a high-scoring game and possibly a one-sided one. Now it settled down to a struggle between fast attack and dogged defense. In teamwork and shooting the two fives were almost evenly matched, and it was only the rangy height of the home team that gave them an advantage. Little by little they pulled ahead. The score favored Roosevelt by 14 to 11 at the quarter—22 to 17 when the half ended.

It had been rugged work all the way and the varsity stretched wearily on the locker-room benches while Brent rubbed them down.

"What are we doin' wrong, Coach?" Gino panted. "There must be some way to beat a big outfit like that."

"You're playing good basketball," said Brent. "I've got no complaints. But remember this. They're just as tired as you are. This second half'll prove which team has the most guts. I'm going to try an experiment when we go out again. We'll put all the height we can muster on the floor. Joe, you'll go in for Ben at guard. Thornton, you'll take Jerry's place. If it doesn't work out we'll just find some other way."

The two teams returned to the court and they could see that the Teddies' line-up was unchanged. Ben was sitting next to Peewee on the bench.

"Watch this," he said. "That guy I was playing against. He's awful tall—six-five or so—but skinny an' not too strong. Wait an' see what happens when he tangles with a rugged guy like Joe Pulaski."

Roosevelt got the tap and moved the ball down with all the assurance they had shown in the first half. But this time when the lanky forward went loping in to shoot he ran into a block by Pulaski that nearly broke him in two. He picked himself up shakily and went to the foul line where he missed both penalty tries. Immediately he was taken out and a smaller man replaced him.

Joe looked sheepishly toward the bench, as much as to say, "Gosh, Coach, I didn't mean to rock him that hard!" But Brent sat there poker-faced, giving no sign either of approval or disapproval. A moment later, as the Hornets went down on the attack, Thornton Sedgely took a pass from Johnny thirty feet out and made one of his one-handed jump shots. It took the Rough Riders by surprise and this time the elongated center was out of position. The whole crowd cheered as the ball dropped through. It was one of those unbelievable shots that people go to basketball games to see.

Brent was on his feet, pacing up and down in front of the bench. "He's got his eye!" they could hear him muttering. "Feed that boy!"

There was no need to tell the boys on the floor. Every time they got their hands on the ball in the next few minutes they maneuvered to get Sedgely into shooting position. And he came through. Twice he fired from outside and scored. Once he was fouled as he drove close to the basket and promptly converted the penalty shot. Meanwhile the Rough Riders had been able to make only one field goal, and midway in the third period the score was tied up at 24 points apiece.

At that juncture the Roosevelt coach called a time-out. Brent gathered the green-jerseyed boys around him.

"I figure they'll put two men on Thornton," he said. "If they do, you might try faking the ball to him and then throwing in to the pivot. Clem, that'll make you the key man. If you see Thornton's clear, feed him. If they're double-guarding him, take your own shot or feed it to anybody who's loose. Have you noticed whether they're slowing down yet?"

"Yes," Johnny Gale answered. "I think they're getting tired." And the others nodded their agreement.

"Good," said Brent. "Keep the pressure on till the end of the quarter. After that I've got another surprise for 'em."

Something the rival coach had told his squad seemed to have stirred them up. They galloped down for a quick goal as soon as play was resumed. But after that the Hornets held them even. Just as Brent had expected, two big men were assigned to bottle up Sedgely, and most of the shooting was done by Clem and Gino. A moment before the period ended Johnny Gale got into the act with a long set shot and the scoreboard showed 34 points for Roosevelt, 33 for Hackersville.

"Some of those big fellows are puffing pretty hard," Brent remarked with a grin when they came back to the bench. "I shouldn't wonder if there'd be some substitutes in there, this last quarter. Well, we're going to make a few changes, too. Ben, I'm going to put you back in and give Johnny a rest. Jerry and Peewee, take over at forwards. How about you, Clem? Getting bushed yet?"

"No, sir, not me," the tall Negro chuckled. "Just nice an' warmed up."

"All right, that's the line-up then. We'll forget about height and concentrate on speed for a while. Clem and Joe'll take care of the rebounding, and Peewee and Jerry'll do the running. You're the two fastest men on the floor. Let's see you prove it!"

Peewee had been building up nervous tension for three quarters, wondering if he would ever get a chance. Now, as he danced out on the floor, the crowd laughed and cheered. He didn't mind. He was used to that kind of a greeting. The Teddies had replaced all their biggest men except the elongated center, and their fresh players set off with a rush. Joe and Ben succeeded in breaking up their first attack. Then Clem took the ball off the backboard after a wild shot and heaved a long pass out to the waiting Peewee.

The little forward took it on the run. He dribbled

down-floor like a miniature hurricane and exploded with a hook shot through the hoop before any Rough Rider could get within five yards of him. The yell that went up from both sides of the floor was spontaneous and deafening.

On the next Roosevelt drive Joe Pulaski tried a steal and as he wrestled for the ball with an opposing forward the referee's whistle shrilled. "Held ball!" he called. "Jump it off."

Jerry and Peewee drifted out toward the sidelines, and a Rough Rider guard hastily followed the small redhead. Roosevelt didn't mean to let him get loose again. On the jump Joe tapped the ball to Greenbaum, who faked toward Peewee, then flipped a long pass out to Jerry. The Irish lad was ready and his race down the floor was as spectacular as Peewee's had been. However, the defenders were more alert this time. The fastest man on their squad got down in time to prevent a shot, and Jerry had to pass out to Clem at the foul line. The Hornet center went through the motions of sending up a one-hander although long arms were waving in his face. For a split second Peewee was left unguarded and Clem's fast bounce pass came straight into his hands. He went up like a jumping-jack. The ball hung on the rim, rolled around once and fell through. The electric lights on the scoreboard changed to 37 for the Hornets. Roosevelt still had 34.

HORNETS
ROOSEVELT
2
ROO
HORNE
10

They never lost that lead. Battling down to the final whistle against a determined team of Rough Riders, they managed to match them goal for goal. There was a lot of scoring in that last quarter, and with only a dozen seconds remaining the Roosevelt pivot man tapped one in to cut the Hornet lead to 46-45. Frantically the Teddies went into a pressing defense, trying to steal the ball. For that moment they forgot all about Peewee, and when the pass from Clem came sailing toward him he was in the clear. His solo sprint wound up in the last goal of the game —his own eleventh point and the forty-eighth for Hackersville.

The line of upstate cars was waiting when they came out of the gym. The five-piece band was playing and Dotty Gordon was leading a cheer on the side-walk. Their progress through the streets of the big town was a parade of triumph—horns tooting, banners waving—and at last they were out on the open high-way.

"Boy, oh, boy!" Mr. Carson kept repeating. "The undefeated Roosevelt Rough Riders! Boy, oh, boy! I nearly busted my vest buttons when you streaked down for that first basket, Son. And that one-hand California jump shot o' yours, Thornton! They're still talking about it. I hope your father was listening."

"He was, all right," Thornton replied. "He wanted to come to the game but Mother and the doctor wouldn't let him. Maybe he can get out to see us play Denton, Saturday night."

Peewee got to bed a little after midnight and was up again next morning in time to cover his route. While they were eating breakfast, his father was chuckling over the morning paper.

"Looks as if they've discovered you, Greg, my boy," he said. "You've got a new nickname, too. Take a look at this." He pointed to a paragraph part way down the column.

"The last quarter," Peewee read, "produced some of the hottest basketball witnessed here in years. A little carrot-topped speedster named Carson broke the game wide open. Local fans will remember him as one of last year's Midget League stars. He hasn't grown much but he can play a lot of forward, and his running and shooting sparked the drive that pulled out a victory for the Hornets. 'Sparky' Carson, they call him, and we'd like to wager you'll hear a lot about Sparky in the future."

The boy finished his breakfast and set off reluctantly for school. It wasn't the cold March wind that made his face red as he went up the steps. He tried to sneak into the classroom unobserved, but a dozen grinning youngsters were there before him.

"Hiya, Sparky!" they greeted him in chorus. And he suddenly discovered he didn't mind, for there was no malice in their voices—only a kind of awed respect.

CHAPTER 15

THAT WAS the first time Peewee had ever known hero-worship, and he wasn't at all sure he liked it. The fact that a big city sports writer had mentioned him favorably seemed to make far too much difference. Actually, as he well knew, his part in beating Roosevelt had been no more commendable than that of any of his team-mates. He felt he deserved a lot less credit than Clem Johnson, for instance, who had played beautifully every minute of the game. But when he tried to put his idea in words, they laughed him down.

"Don't go modest on us, Sparky," said Ben Greenbaum. "We'd still be a second-division club if it wasn't for you."

Peewee shook his head. "You're nuts," he replied

unhappily. "The team was due, this year. I admit Thornton's helped, but if I'd stayed in the city you'd have been up with the leaders just the same."

Only Elmer Brent seemed to understand his point of view. "You're probably right, Peewee," the coach told him. "But if they want to make a hero of you, let 'em. After all, it's good for their morale to have a sort of mascot, and I guess you're it."

The evening paper helped to deflate the balloon a little. Digging into his files, the editor had come up with the picture of Peewee standing under Clem Johnson's arm. It was featured in two columns on the first sports page, with the caption, "Long and short of Hornets' offense." The story of the game mentioned the little forward, but only as one of the team members who had worked together to pull a real David-and-Goliath upset.

There was no practice that afternoon, but on Thursday Brent had them on the floor early. "Okay, gang," he told them, "it's time to get the stars out of our eyes and think about just one thing—beating Denton. Maybe some of you have forgotten the licking they gave us in December. Well, I haven't. I heard a lot of talk then about how we were robbed—how we'd really be laying for 'em when they came to Hackersville. Maybe that was just talk. Anyhow, they'll be here Saturday night, and after what we did to Roosevelt they'll be out for blood How about it—practice, anybody?"

They settled down to fundamentals—shooting, passing, and defense—and there was no skylarking now. At the end of half an hour Brent lined them up for scrimmage.

"I did a little scouting last night," he said. "Went over to Raymond, where Denton was playing the Redwings. Denton won, 48 to 46, but they looked better than that. Remember Whaley, that tall center of theirs? He's improved plenty since we played 'em. He scored twenty-one points and his work off the backboard was really hot. Clem's going to have his hands full with that boy, and if the rest of their team was as good we wouldn't have a chance. Fortunately there are some weak spots in their defense. Half the time they don't seem to know whether they're using man-to-man or zone. They keep shifting, and when they do that there's usually an opening for a smart attack. I want you to be ready for those chances."

The second team had orders to shuttle back and forth, first guarding man-to-man, then dropping back into a zone defense. And nearly every time they tried it one of the varsity players succeeded in getting off a shot.

They had another good work-out Friday and everything was ready for the final game on the schedule. Not much else was talked about in Hackersville that weekend. Denton's season record of fourteen wins and three losses was almost identical with the Hornets' thirteen and two. Both teams were pretty certain to be picked for the regional play-offs. And for Hackersville rooters there was the added desire to see their school avenge its earlier defeat.

The gymnasium was far too small to hold all those who wanted to get in, and by seven o'clock every seat and every inch of standing room was filled. The Denton radio station had sent over a play-by-play announcer and set up broadcasting facilities in the balcony, and two sports reporters from the city shared the tiny "press section" with the *Clarion's* man.

Keeping the crowd happy for an hour had left the band breathless and the cheer-leaders hoarse by the time the teams came on the floor. Between warm-up shots Peewee looked around for friends in the stand. He located his father and Jane without difficulty, and just behind them he saw Mr. and Mrs. Sedgely. He was a little shocked to see how thin and worn Thornton's father looked. But he could still smile. Mrs. Sedgely, pretty and vivacious as ever, waved her hand to Peewee and as he waved back he almost fell over. For sitting beside her was his own mother! None of the arguments they had offered at suppertime had succeeded in persuading her to come. He thought Mrs. Sedgely must have worked some kind of magic to get her to the game.

Before the start Brent called them into the usual huddle at the bench. "We're going to alternate two

sets of forwards," he said. "Gino and Jerry'll start, and play the full first period. Then Thornton and Peewee go in for the second quarter, and so on. Get away fast and keep the pressure on 'em. And watch for holes in their defense. Good luck!"

The Denton five looked pretty confident as they faced off for the jump. They had snickered a few times at the size of the gym when they first came out, but now they were all business. The whistle blew and the referee tossed up the ball. Clem made a mighty jump but the long-legged Whaley reached an inch or two higher and got the tap. The Hornet defense formed quickly. They blocked any immediate tries for the basket, but after half a minute of ball-handling there was a pass in to Whaley at the pivot. His lay-up was good.

Hackersville came back quickly on a hook shot by Gino. A foul was called on Jerry as he tried to steal the ball on the way down-floor and the Denton guard converted it for a point. Ten seconds later Clem tossed in a smooth one-hander and the score was 4 to 3.

For the rest of the quarter there was no marked advantage on either side. The two teams scored, turn and turn about, and the shooting average was good for both fives. Off the backboards Clem didn't have his usual edge, for he was playing against one of the top centers in the state. However, he recovered his share of rebounds, and his work in the pivot spot was close to perfection.

The eight-minute period ended with the tally tied at 11 to 11. Peewee and Thornton stripped off their sweat suits and pranced up and down to limber their legs while the home crowd cheered.

"Let's have a little more speed out there," Brent counseled. "This thing could go on all night unless we break it up. Make 'em run, this next quarter."

The two new forwards reported at the scorer's table, then came back to the bench for a quick huddle before the team took the floor. It was Denton's ball outside, and their guards worked it in cautiously, hunting for an opening. Finally they found a forward loose. He took the pass and tried for a quick one, but his shot went wide, bouncing far out off the board. Johnny Gale was there to take it.

"Peewee!" he yelled, and let fly with a long pass. The little forward had started sprinting when he saw the angle of the shot. He was clear of the pack when he caught the ball, and his fast break took him under the basket well ahead of the nearest defender. Timing his hook nicely he sent the ball up and through to the accompaniment of wild cheering from the stands.

That goal produced the result Brent had wanted. It opened the game up and started both teams moving faster.

Before the Denton squad recovered its poise Thornton added two more points with a leaping one-hand shot from outside that brought the fans to their feet. And the Hornets succeeded in holding that margin right up to the half-time whistle. When they left the floor the score stood Hackersville 23, Denton 19.

Brent knew the first-string forwards must be smarting a little because their replacements had put the team in front. However, he didn't rub it in.

"This third quarter belongs to you and Jerry, Gino," he said. "They're behind and they'll be making a big try, but if you keep the pressure on you'll stay ahead. Show 'em some *real* speed!"

Then he turned to Ben and Johnny. "That number three play ought to click about now. They'll be concentrating on offense, and if their guarding gets sloppy it'll be easier for Clem. I'll be watching from the bench and I'll rub the top of my head to let you know when."

The varsity players got off fast after the jump, and though Denton scored first, Gino hung one up from the corner to match their two-pointer. The visitors swarmed around the basket, firing wildly, shot after shot. When Clem finally recovered a rebound, the coach rubbed vigorously at his hair and Johnny Gale nodded to show he had caught the signal.

There was no chance for a fast break, for the Denton players were rushing helter-skelter toward their own basket. Johnny and Ben brought the ball down and Clem eased into the pivot. They worked the ball around the pattern once or twice while the defense milled back and forth in confusion. Then Ben shouted to draw attention to himself. He took Gino's pass, bounced it once and faked a cut to the right. Three Denton men, including the rangy center, lunged to block his path. His hand-off to Clem was perfectly timed. With the defense still off balance the pivot man whirled and laid up a beauty to give the Hornets a six-point lead.

A time-out was called by the opposite bench, and when the Denton team returned to the court there was a difference in the tempo of the game. Evidently they had been told to control the ball. It was a full minute before they took a shot and Jerry Donovan got over-anxious. He was called for hacking just as the opposing forward let fly at the basket. It went through and the Denton man made good on his foul try, picking up three points.

Neither side could gain an advantage in the next few minutes. Hackersville tried to speed it up, but Denton continued to play cautiously. They alternated on field goals and when Jerry tried a steal he was rapped for another foul. Luckily the Denton guard missed both his shots. The score at the three-quarter mark was 33 to 30 in the Hornets' favor.

"Nice job, boys," Brent told them. "They'll probably stick to their slow game awhile longer, but I look for 'em to start some firehouse basketball toward the end if we're still in the lead. Anyhow, you'll know what to do. When they start pressing we may get some chances at the foul line. How's your eye, Peewee?"

The little forward grinned. "Okay, I hope—if they don't beat on me too hard, that is."

They pulled the "number three" play again in the final period, and Peewee boosted his own scoring total by a set shot and a fast break lay-up. Denton, meanwhile, was controlling the ball doggedly on the attack and shooting with more accuracy. They still trailed by only three points when the referee announced that the three-minute rule was in effect.

Hackersville brought the ball out. Johnny and Ben

passed carefully, watching for something to happen. And it did. Two new guards had come in for the visitors. Before the Hornet veterans could get over the center line the whole Denton team came charging up-floor in a close press, bent on getting that ball.

Johnny sidestepped coolly and fired a low-bounce pass under the crowding arms. It went to Peewee, who rifled to Thornton. And the California boy went into the air with his specialty—a kangaroo one-hander that sailed true.

From that moment there was no more doubt about the outcome. The Hornets tantalized the frantic Denton defenders by what looked like freezing tactics, and the fouls followed inevitably. Twice in those last three minutes Peewee stood on the fifteen-foot line, groggy from being knocked down. But his head cleared each time and he sank both double-headers for four big points. When the last whistle blew, Hackersville had won its fourteenth game and revenged its earlier Denton defeat by the solid score of 49 to 38.

There was bedlam in the little gymnasium after that. The green-shirted squad couldn't get to the locker-room for ten minutes. Fathers, mothers, brothers and sisters swarmed all over the players, laughing and shouting themselves hoarse. An arm in a green sweater was flung around Peewee's neck and he was kissed soundly on the cheek. When he turned his head he found Dotty Gordon's smiling eyes looking into his own.

"Sparky," she said, "you were just wonderful! And don't get so red-faced. It doesn't match your hair. Hi, Mrs. Carson! Aren't you glad you came?"

Peewee's mother had worked her way through the mob to his side. She was beaming.

"I wouldn't have missed it for anything, Dotty," she told the girl. "Thanks for making me change my mind. How do you feel, Greg? Those big boys were banging into you pretty hard."

"Aw, gosh, Mom!" he said. "Don't worry about that. I can take care o' myself. I'm awful glad you decided to come, though. Maybe we'll make a fan out of you yet!"

As Dotty left, Thornton Sedgely and his mother joined them. The boy looked happier than Peewee had seen him in all the many weeks since his father was hurt.

"Evening, Mrs. Carson," he said with a grin. "Look, Peewee—why don't you all come over to our house? We'll have an end-of-the-season celebration!"

"Please do," Mrs. Sedgely urged. "We'd love to have you."

Peewee's mother hesitated. "Are you sure it wouldn't be too much for your husband?" she asked doubtfully.

"I think it would do him good," the other woman

smiled. "As a matter of fact he was the one who suggested it! See if you can get Jane and Mr. Brent to come along, too."

The boys hurried off to shower and dress, and half an hour later the two families were gathered in the big living room of the Hacker mansion. Mr. Sedgely sat in a deep lounging chair near the open fire.

"This is the best home-coming I could have," he told them with a smile. "Watching you win that game made me feel better than all the medicine the doctors have been giving me."

CHAPTER 16

THE PARTY lasted till after eleven that night. Mrs. Sedgely served them refreshments and the men and boys talked steadily about basketball.

"What do you think of this team now, Coach?" Mr. Carson asked.

Elmer Brent laughed. "I'll have to be honest with you," he said. "Back in November I thought we'd have a good season. I figured with the experience the boys had we could win more than half our games, and that's all anybody can ask from a little school like ours. The one thing that worried me was depth. If anything happened to the first team I knew we'd be sunk.

"And then," he chuckled, "along came some luck.

Right at the start of the season I found I had two new players about as good as the veterans. If they came through for us I had a hunch it would really make the team. And they have. We can count on eight good men now—because having Thornton around has made Joe Pulaski work harder and polish up his game. But the thing that's made us click is having two good sets of forwards. You saw it work tonight. Put that speed in front of a pair of smart, steady guards like Johnny and Ben, and a top-notch center like Clem, and you've got a nice scoring machine."

"What about the Regionals that start next week?" Peewee's father asked. "Think you've got a chance?"

"I'd rather not be quoted," Brent laughed. "Getting into 'em is what I've been trying for. Now that we're in we'll just play one game at a time and do our best."

The Carsons were on their way home that evening when Peewee's mother spoke up from the back seat. "I declare, Gregory," she said, "I guess it's a good thing I went to that game. I never would have known what a poor job I did on those sweat pants if I hadn't seen you wearing 'em. I must have shortened 'em too much—and the other boys looked so nice and neat. Don't forget now. You bring those pants home from school and let me fix 'em. They ought to be dry-cleaned, too, before you play anywhere again."

Peewee laughed. "You're wonderful, Mom," he

said. "Had your eye glued to those pants, but I bet you didn't see me score a single point!"

He did remember to bring the sweat pants home on Monday. He pulled them on over his clothes and stood in front of the long mirror in Jane's room. There was an undeniable gap of an inch or two between the bottoms of the pants and his shoes.

He took them down to his mother. "Must be cheap stuff," he said. "They looked all right when you first fixed 'em. I guess they've shrunk."

That afternoon Coach Brent had called them together before practice. "In case you haven't seen it in the papers," he told the squad, "the four teams in the Regionals are Denton, Randall, Allerton—and us. We know something about Denton and Allerton. Randall we haven't seen yet, but they've got a good record—fifteen and four for the season. The play-offs will be next Friday and Saturday in the armory at Randall. It's a pretty good floor and it'll seat six or seven thousand people. I don't know who we play first. The draw won't be made till tomorrow. Any questions?"

"Yes," said Johnny Gale. "Can you fix it so we get a shot at Allerton?"

Brent smiled and shook his head. "I know how you feel," he answered. "But whether we play them depends on the luck of the draw."

The captain's question was at least partially answered on Tuesday, when the evening papers carried the regional pairings. Hackersville was to meet the Randall Ramblers in the semi-final round, while Denton tangled with Allerton. On the same sport page there were season records of all the regional teams. Eagerly the boys studied the Ramblers' won and lost column. They had played only three schools that were on the Hornets' schedule. Their victories over Red Creek and Clay City were by fairly big scores. On the other hand they had been nosed out by Franklin Tech, losing 52 to 49.

At Wednesday's practice Elmer Brent was able to tell them more about their opening opponents.

"I called up the coach at Clay City last night," he said. "Without having had a chance to scout Randall myself, I wanted his opinion. Well, the news is bad. He says they're the best-balanced team he's seen all year. A light team, fast, with no very tall men but some real ball hawks. Their shooting star is a forward named Farley. He's averaged over 20 points a game for the season and hit 32 on his best night."

"What do we do, Coach—put two men on him?" Johnny Gale asked.

"We may have to, though Clay City tried it and got no place. What I'd like to try first is a regular man-to-man defense and a bang-bang offense—see if we can't outscore the guy. Thornton, you'll have to pretend you're Mr. Ace Farley in this scrimmage. He usually works in the pivot, by the way, and he favors twisting one-handers.''

Sedgely carried out the assignment so well that the second team had a lead after five minutes and the varsity was worried.

Brent grinned. "Okay," he told them, "try a collapsing zone defense. Fall back down the middle and clog up that alley when they feed him the ball."

The new strategy reduced the number of pivot shots Thornton was able to make, and the second-stringers had to switch their attack. Peewee began clicking with set shots from outside, forcing the varsity to open up the defense once more. All in all it was a lively practice, but it proved little about the best method of stopping a scoring ace.

"I guess," said Ben Greenbaum, "we'll just have to play it by ear when we get out on the floor with 'em."

Peewee was still thinking about the the legendary Farley when they were dressing. "Clem," he asked the tall center, "what's your point average for the season?"

The Negro boy chuckled. "Haven't any idea," he said. "I guess in a little old country high school like this nobody bothers to figure such things. Mebbe that's good. We don't need stars, jus' so we win games."

Peewee knew it was a sensible answer but his curiosity remained. He met Speck Newbury in the corridor as he was leaving and asked the manager if he had ever worked out scoring averages for the different players.

Speck looked at him owlishly. "It's odd you should ask," he replied. "I happen to have them right here. The sports editor at the *Clarion* wanted them tonight."

Peewee ran his eye quickly down the list. As he had expected, Clem Johnson led with an average of 17 points. Marchetti and Donovan had 12 and 11.5 respectively. Gale and Greenbaum stood at 9.4 and 10.1. Surprising to him was the fact that he himself had averaged 8 points for the season, while Sedgely was close behind with 7.6.

He mentioned the figures at supper that night. His father didn't seem much impressed.

"No George Mikans in that bunch," Mr. Carson laughed. "I'd have guessed your average was higher than eight points."

"Maybe it ought to be," Peewee returned, "but Thornton and I have played less'n half time in most games. As for stars, which would you rather have—one twenty-five point man or five twelve-point men?"

"Hmm." His father scratched his chin. "Yes—you've got something there. Maybe I don't need to worry about this Randall High star I've been reading about. What's his name—Farley?"

*   *   *

"Rrr-ah! Rrr-ah! Rrr-ah! Far-ley!"
The cheer rang back from the naked steel rafters of

the armory and echoed in the ears of the Hornets as they ran out on the floor. Theirs was the second game of the night—the big one for the home-town Randall rooters. Allerton had already put Denton out of the running in the earlier game, part of which the Hornet squad had been able to watch.

"Farley?" said Gino, taking the ball from Johnny and going in for a lay-up. "Who's he?"

"Never saw him," Ben replied, making his own shot. "But I'm sure I don't like the guy."

Clem laid one up with a soft *whoosh.* "Tell you who he is," he grinned. "He's the feller that's standin' between us an' another crack at those Allerton Tigers— that's all!"

The rapid fire of talk was good for their nerves. They were loose and hot when the whistle blew, eager as a bunch of terriers. Brent started the regulars, but Pee-wee and Thornton knew they wouldn't stay on the bench long.

"There he is," Peewee whispered. "The blond guy —number six."

Farley wasn't especially tall, but he moved with a smooth-muscled grace that was pretty to watch. He slipped easily into the slot, took a quick pass, twisted as he jumped, and floated a hook shot through the cords. The jubilant roar of the crowd drowned out any remarks on the Hornet bench, but the boys looked at each other in some dismay.

196

"Whew!" Thornton breathed. "He's like a cat! Now I can see where he got the name of Easy Ed Farley."

The Hornets worked the ball down quickly, eager to rack up a score of their own. But the defense was tight. When Gino finally found daylight for a try, his shot missed the hoop by inches and a Randall guard recovered. There was a race for the opposite basket. Clem and Johnny got to the keyhole a step ahead of the fast-moving Farley and teamed up on him, leaving

the other three Hornets to cover four attackers as best they could. The cordon was too thin. It wasn't long before the Rambler center broke through and dropped in a lay-up shot.

Twenty seconds later Jerry Donovan got a bit too aggressive and was called for charging. The converted foul try gave the home team five big points and Brent asked for time out.

"Take it easy, gang," he told them. "Just go out there and start over. Remember we've got a pretty good scoring punch of our own. Feed Clem this time. Once they start worrying about stopping *our* hot man, you can pour on the speed and even things up in a hurry."

They had been tense and frowning. Now they re-laxed. Back on the floor, Johnny and Ben brought the ball down, zipped it once around the pattern and into Gino's hands. He faked a cut, passed high and straight to Clem, in the slot, and the big boy's pivot shot went in. The cheers this time came from the visitors' side.

Randall tried a fast break and Ben Greenbaum—"the Brain"—was waiting for it. He snared the ball out of the air. Before the opposition could back-track, his dribble carried him under the basket and his lay-up was good. The Hornet defense continued to bottle up Farley, but this time it was Johnny and Ben who did the guarding. Clem Johnson, covering the Randall center, took one off the backboard. His long, arching pass found Jerry Donovan, halfway down the floor and under full steam. The fiery little forward never missed a stride. He hooked from ten feet out and the shot put Hackersville in the lead for the first time.

At the end of the first quarter it was still a tight game, with the Hornets ahead by 13 to 12.

"Here goes our one-two punch," said Elmer Brent with a grin. "Peewee and Thornton take over. But don't underestimate this Farley guy. He's scored half their points, even with two men on him."

The Randall players looked a little puzzled as they faced the new Hornet forwards. Their own line-up was unchanged. Bringing the ball in to start the period they went into a controlled offense, moving first one man and then another into the pivot. The maneuver was meant to shake Farley loose, but Ben and Johnny stuck to him like leeches. It was only when he drifted back, out of the pattern, that they broke away.

Peewee sensed what was coming even before the pass was thrown to the Rambler star. He got there fast and jumped as high as he could, but the set shot went over his reaching fingertips—a thirty-five-footer that dropped straight through the hoop.

The Hornets clenched their teeth and started over while the home-town crowd went wild. The defense was concentrating on Clem Johnson. Peewee faked a pass to the pivot, then cut to the left and handed off to Thornton. The California boy went up with his specialty—the one-hand jump shot—and Hackersville was in front once more.

Within half a minute Peewee got into the scoring column on a rebound and a fast break. Then, when Randall lost the ball for traveling, the little redhead tossed in a set shot almost as long as Farley's. And before the Ramblers could find the range again, Clem hit with a lay-up and converted a foul try to make the tally 22 to 14.

The rapid-fire scoring upset the smooth team play of the Randall five. They looked ragged on defense and their passing and shooting fell off. Before more damage could be done their coach called time. There were still four minutes left in the quarter, and Brent told his boys to keep the pressure on.

The Ramblers had pulled themselves together during the breather. They came down cautiously, giving the pattern time to develop. And again it was Ed Farley who broke the ice on a neat give-and-go play. Johnny Gale, trying to stop him, accidentally hacked his arm on the shot, and the star added another point from the foul line. After that his team attacked with more confidence. The Hornets were lucky to hold onto a 5-point lead at the intermission.

Hackersville's two-platoon system paid off in the second half, for the fresh sets of forwards kept the pace fast. Even Farley showed signs of tiring before it was over, though he had a total of 21 points out of his team's 40. The Hornets wound up with 52 and a solid victory.

It was nearly eleven by the time they had showered and dressed, and after midnight before they reached home.

"Get yourselves a good night's sleep," Brent told the squad. "You farm boys—let the old man do the milking and stay in bed as long as you can. The Allerton game starts at three o'clock tomorrow afternoon, so don't eat too big a lunch."

Peewee was too keyed up to go to sleep at once. He went back over the game, play by play, trying to figure where he could have done better. After all, he decided, it hadn't been a bad evening's work. In 16 minutes he had scored 13 points—runner-up to Clem Johnson, who had tallied an even 20. Maybe tomorrow, against the Allerton Tigers, he could improve on that performance.

CHAPTER 17

It HAD BEEN five weeks since the snowy night when the team lost to Allerton, but the defeat still rankled. The hope of getting another crack at the Tigers had spurred every man on the squad to greater effort.

As they put on their suits in the armory that Saturday afternoon, Peewee knew they were too tense, too anxious. Elmer Brent must have sensed it, too, for he tried deliberately to kid them out of it.

"Good thing you've got a coach along this time," he laughed. "I've got no fault to find with the way you played 'em before, but at least you can blame me if anything goes wrong. So relax! They're big—sure—but if we outrun 'em and outshoot 'em their size is just a handicap."

The practice under the basket helped to loosen them up. Somehow the Tigers didn't look quite as formidable this time when the varsity lined up against them. Clem Johnson outjumped their six-foot-six center and slapped the ball over to Gino. Two passes, a fast cut by Jerry, a hand-off to Clem, in the pivot, and the green team had first blood.

They never let up. Johnny's floor work was inspired, and the forwards ran the legs off their husky opponents. At the quarter they came off the floor panting but grinning, proud of their 14 to 8 lead.

"All right, hot-shots," said Gino to Peewee and Thornton, "let's see you do that good!"

Clem had 8 of the 14 points, and as soon as play started again it was evident that the Tigers were going to make it tough for him. Two of their biggest men were assigned to keep him covered, and in the first three minutes the only shot he got at the basket was on a foul. Meanwhile Allerton had struck a hot streak of its own. Three straight field goals put them only a point behind.

Johnny Gale looked at the bench, but Brent didn't call for time. This was one he wanted them to work out for themselves. Ben cut close to the captain as they brought the ball out. He said a quick word or two and Johnny nodded. Then they were in the pattern and Peewee saw some kind of a sign passed to Thornton. Clem was in his usual pivot spot beside the foul lane,

yelling and gesturing for the ball, while the two big
Tiger guards stuck close to his sides. As Greenbaum
faked to Clem, the California boy drifted across, took
a high, hard pass and went up with a perfectly timed
jump to lay it in.

The tide turned again with that shot. Thrown off
balance, the Tigers began firing wild ones at the board,
and Clem, steady as ever, recovered rebound after rebound. At the same time Thornton and Peewee had
found their shooting eyes.

With their home-town team out of the running, the
Randall fans had switched their allegiance to the little
green five. Now, as the Hornets poured in the baskets,
they rocked the armory with a mounting wave of sound.
Organized cheering was lost in that tumult. Dotty Gordon and her yell-leaders gave up the effort and jumped
up and down on the sidelines, screaming with the rest.
The first half ended with Hackersville ahead by the
lopsided score of 34 to 18.

Elmer Brent tried to tone down their exuberance,
back in the dressing room. "You've had a run of luck,"
he said. "And the breaks can swing the other way just
as fast. Those Tigers are going to be a lot tougher from
now on, so don't get the idea this is in the bag. I want
you to play a control game for a while. Hold their scoring down and don't risk a shot till you're sure."

Jerry and Gino looked disappointed but they had
faith in their coach. They played it according to orders

for the first five minutes, while the aroused Tigers barreled up and down the floor trying to get a scoring spree
started. Then, with the board showing 37 to 25, Jerry
got ambitious. Breaking the pattern he cut in and tried
a spectacular jump shot from twenty feet away. The
tall Allerton center was in position, close to the basket,
and he slapped the ball out to mid-court where a racing
forward recovered it. He was all alone when he flipped
in the easy lay-up.

The Irish boy's face showed that he knew he had
been wrong. But in trying to make up for the mistake
he dribbled down too fast and lost the ball as it spurted
over the sideline. The Tigers brought it in and
promptly hit with another two-pointer.

Brent frowned. "Get your sweat pants off, Carson,"
he directed. "I'm afraid Donovan's had it."

The sight of Peewee getting ready must have sobered
Jerry, for he played more cautiously for the next two
minutes. Each team scored one more goal in the quarter, and it ended with Hackersville still on top by
eight points, 39 to 31.

"What do you say, Coach?" Johnny Gale pleaded.
"Can't we take the wraps off now? I bet we're fresher
than they are, an' I know we can outshoot 'em."

Brent hesitated. "All right," he said. "Just don't give
'em too many scoring chances. If they should get really
hot, eight points isn't much of a lead."

The final quarter was under way, but the Hornet

attack couldn't seem to get started. The Tigers had caught fire. They scored on a cleverly executed give-and-go play, then on a long set shot. A foul, called against Ben Greenbaum, whittled the lead down to a slim three points, and Elmer Brent called a time-out.

"Do you know what's happening?" he asked them grimly. "You're getting licked. I thought you wanted to cut loose! Now you've *got* to, if you want to win, because there's too much time left for a freeze. You know the plays. Let's see you use 'em!"

Still smarting under the words, they brought the ball down. Peewee foot-faked past one defender and passed to Sedgely, who fed the ball in to Clem. The big Negro pivoted and connected. On the next Tiger attack he broke up a play under the basket and heaved a long one out to Thornton. The Californian was covered before he could shoot, but a bounce pass to Peewee resulted in another score. Fouled on the shot, the little redhead caged his first try and they had their 8-point lead once more.

"All right, gang," said Johnny Gale. "They'll never catch us now. Let's show 'em some basketball!"

Allerton scored first, but the Hornets came right back with a long set shot by Greenbaum. Thornton laid in a jump one-hander and the three-minute rule went into effect. From then on it turned into a slaughter. The enraged Tigers fouled repeatedly in their efforts to get the ball, and the boys in green were deadly

from the line. As the end neared, with the score 57 to
40 in the Hornets' favor, Clem recovered a rebound
and passed out to Peewee. He glanced at the big clock.
Two seconds left! From 65 feet out he drew back his
arm and uncorked a long heave that arched high above
the court, kissed the backboard and dropped unbelievably through the cords. The buzzer sounded at the same
instant and the game was over.

Mr. Carson was still too excited to be coherent when
Peewee got into the car.

"My gosh, Son!" he chuckled. "That last one—did
you have to rub it in like that? Anyhow, I was proud
of you. Regional champs! Wow!"

*   *   *

The Sunday papers carried a full column on the
game next morning. Under an action picture of Clem
grabbing a rebound away from three Allerton players
the headline read: "TIGERS CRUSHED IN 59-40 UPSET."
And the story played up the drama of the little country
team from Hackersville knocking mighty Allerton out
of the Mid-State finals.

"As usual," the report of the game concluded, "the
versatile Clem Johnson starred for the Hornets. His
21 points topped both teams. The big center isn't the
only star on this Cinderella outfit, however. A pair of
youngsters named Sedgely and Carson, playing only
half the game, scored an even dozen points apiece, and

one of little Carson's shots traveled three-quarters of the length of the floor."

Hackersville was mentioned on other pages as well. "The regional winners, heading this way for the State Championships next week," one sports columnist wrote, "are probably feeling thankful they won't have to meet those big ferocious Tigers. This is just one man's warning that they'd better look again. The way the Hornets keep on winning games is no accident. It's about time they were taken seriously."

The boys were in the locker-room getting into their uniforms when the flare-up came. Joe Pulaski strolled in with his hands in his pockets and stood glowering down at them.

"Come on, Joe," Johnny Gale urged. "Get your suit on. We'll be starting in a couple o' minutes."

The big Polish boy gave him a sour grin and shook his head. "Not me," he said. "You hot-shots that do all the playin' an' get the write-ups in the papers can practice if you want to. Me—I'm quittin'."

They sat there, too shocked by the suddenness of it to answer. Then Peewee saw a figure standing in the doorway. Elmer Brent walked in. There were tight lines around his mouth and they could feel the anger in him. Nobody moved or spoke.

"All right, Joe," he said quietly. "I heard what you said, and I can't say I blame you. I'd like to burn every sports page that comes into this town before anybody

208

has a chance to read it. I've told all of you before, and I'm saying it again now—there are no stars on this squad. We've been winning games because we were a team."

He paused to let the words sink in. "Now," he went on, "I've got some news for you. The University has scheduled a game for the Field House Friday night. That means the state high school semi-finals and finals will all have to be played on Saturday. There'll be two games in the afternoon between the regional champions. The two winners will play for the title in the evening. If we're lucky enough to get through the semi-final round we'll have to be out there on the floor again at eight o'clock, fighting for the big one. I wouldn't ask any of you to play two full games of basketball in five or six hours. So I expect to use every man on the squad. That includes you, Joe, and Ray and Jack and Jim. Any questions?"

There were no questions. Big Joe took off his jacket without a word and hung it in his locker. He was in his basketball clothes and taking practice shots almost as soon as the others.

They played hard and with purpose that day and every day throughout the week. The coach's words had given fresh incentive to the substitutes. And Brent kept shifting them around—using new combinations that gave every man a chance to show what he could do.

Sometimes Peewee was playing with the original varsity, sometimes on a team that included only one or two of the first-string men. He was tried at guard as well as forward, and once he even found himself working in the pivot spot for a few minutes. The teamwork of these pick-up combinations was ragged at first. But gradually they reached a point where each man knew how to play with any four of the others.

"Most coaches," Brent told them with a grin, "would say I was crazy to be doing this. They'd want to polish up one team. If it doesn't work I'll be the world's biggest chump, but I'm going to stay with the plan."

For all the fire they put into those practice games there was little fouling. The coach had cautioned them against roughness.

"With a squad the size of ours," he said, "we can't afford to have even one man hurt. That goes for sickness, too. Eat right, get plenty of sleep and stay away from people with colds."

It was hard on Joe Pulaski to avoid using his strength in tight spots, but he was good-natured about it and kept himself under control. Day by day he was playing a better game, smoother on the rebounds, faster and more accurate on the shots and passes. He watched Clem and did his best to copy the tall Negro boy's easy style.

Following Brent's orders, they avoided reading the sports pages that week. Peewee's father reveled in the columns of type that were devoted to the four teams in the state championships, but the boy refused to listen to his comments.

"The coach says those guys make up half of what they write," he explained. "They do more harm than good, building up stars. What he wants us to do is go after one game at a time, just like we have all season, and forget about the wonder boys on the other team."

The pairings were announced on Wednesday. Franklin Tech, which had clinched the Metropolitan Regional championship by beating Roosevelt in a play-off, would be meeting Bellwood in one semi-final. Pee-wee had heard of the Bellwood Bombers before. Their smooth-playing team from a big residential suburb had won the Northwest Regionals without dropping a game all season.

In the other afternoon game the Hornets would face the rugged Steelville Iron Men, winners of the North-east title.

Big Joe rubbed his hands at that news. "Those guys are my meat," he chuckled. "They like to play rough. Goin' to give me a shot at 'em, Coach?"

Brent nodded. "I told you you'd get your chance," he said. "You may not start but you'll see all the action you want. A lot of things depend on which game comes first. That won't be decided till Saturday, when we get to the Field House."

They had a light practice Friday, concentrating on floor plays and sharpening up their shooting. When it was over they packed their uniforms for the trip.

Peewee went to bed at nine but lay tossing and turn-ing for the next hour. He was keyed up to a tighter pitch than he had been in months. This was it—the incredible season's finish that he hadn't allowed him-self even to dream about—and he was nervous as a cat. Finally he went down to the kitchen and drank a glass of warm milk. It helped him settle down and in another five minutes he was asleep.

Saturday turned out to be a fine spring day and Hackersville was in a gala mood. All morning the cars streamed out of town on their way to the city.

The Carsons got away by ten o'clock. Peewee rode with his father and mother while Jane, as usual, was in Elmer Brent's car. Before noon they were inching through downtown traffic and as soon as a parking place could be found they went to a restaurant for lunch. Peewee ate lightly, according to orders. It wasn't difficult, for he had an uneasy feeling in his stomach—the "butterflies" that even professional athletes are likely to get before a big game.

An hour later they pulled into the big parking lot that flanked the University Field House. Surprisingly there were already a lot of cars there and crowds were standing in line at the ticket windows. Peewee found the coach with some of the boys and they waited till the whole squad had assembled. Then Speck Newbury turned up with the team passes. In a sober file they went through the gate and into the huge building.

CHAPTER 18

AT ONE-THIRTY the coaches and captains of the four
teams were called to a conference in the Athletic Di-
rector's office. Meanwhile the Hornet squad sat together in a corner of the big locker-room and waited.
They talked in low voices, kidding each other a little,
trying to keep from showing their nervousness.

When Johnny Gale came back he was grinning.
"Okay, gang," he said, "you can climb into your suits.
We got a break on the toss. Our game's at two-thirty.
I'd hate to have it the other way—sweating it out for
another couple of hours!"

His news helped to relieve the tension. Now that
they knew they wouldn't have to wait the boys could
laugh again. They got into their clean uniforms and

sweat suits and at two o'clock Brent came to tell them it was time to go out on the floor.

Several thousand people were already in their seats and more kept filtering into the great arena every minute. The coach followed the team up the ramp, his arms full of basketballs.

"Maybe some of you remember what I said back in January," he told them. "Before the Franklin game I made the crack that you'd better get used to playing here—because this is where the state finals would be held. It sounded a bit silly then, but I had a hunch. And you've made it come true. Let's see some nice shooting now. When you come back to the bench I'll tell you who's going to start."

They heard a shrill Hackersville cheer as they trotted over to the basket and the home-town band, pieced out by several instruments from the Legion Post, struck up *Fight, You Hornets, Fight!*

Peewee, at the tail of the circle, had time to look around the stands for his parents before it was his turn to shoot. He finally spotted them, right in the middle of the Hackersville rooting section. Then there was more cheering and the gray-suited Steelville squad came pounding out at the opposite end of the court.

Peewee took his shot and stole a look at the enemy. They were big, powerful youngsters, built along the same lines as the Red Creek Miners. They had sixteen men in uniform and their practice shots seemed to be falling in with monotonous regularity.

Promptly at two twenty-five the officials whistled the two teams back to their benches. Brent had a piece of paper in his hand. "Here's the starting line-up I've given the scorekeeper," he said. "Gale and Greenbaum, guards; Johnson, center; Donovan and Marchetti, forwards. I'll be putting in subs early and often."

Some of the second-stringers looked a little downcast at the announcement, but nobody could really quarrel with the idea of starting the five veterans. They had earned it.

"This game," the coach continued, "may be decided on fouls. Steelville plays a rough game and they get away with it up in their country. I doubt if they can here. Let's keep it clean and see what happens. And when you get a penalty shot, make it count!"

The loudspeakers were blaring out the names of the starting fives. The Hornets went into a quick huddle, gripped hands all 'round, and took their places on the floor. Peewee drew a deep breath as they waited for the whistle.

The Iron Man center looked enormous standing beside Clem Johnson. According to the score-card he was twenty years old, stood six-nine and weighed two hundred and twenty pounds. On the jump, however, it was Clem who got the tap. The ball went to Johnny, who faked a long pass and bounced to Ben. The guard dribbled down the sideline, fired across to Gino in the corner, and the Italian boy looped a perfect one-hander into the basket.

Less than a minute later the tall Steelville center laid one up to tie the score and the Hornets brought it down again. This time the going was harder. Under a pressing defense they worked the ball around the pattern, waiting for a break. Johnny faked his man off balance for a second and passed high to Clem, in the slot. The pivot man went up for his shot and was shoved as it left his hand. Instantly the whistle blew.

"Foul on six!" the referee called. "Two shots."

Clem smiled and took his stance at the line. He floated the ball up like thistledown and put both shots in. Immediately the Iron Men were galloping goalward like a troop of cavalry. One big forward ran right over Ben Greenbaum and the whistle sounded again.

"Charging," said the referee. "Foul on three. One plus one."

There were angry shouts from Steelville supporters in the stands. Ben picked himself up and walked slowly to the other end of the floor. He looked shaky and his first try missed the hoop by a foot. They could see him trying to pull himself together as he bounced the ball. This time it went in.

The 5-2 lead lasted only a few seconds. Steelville scored on another lay-up by the center, then went ahead on a long one from outside. Jerry stole the ball

on the next play, but was fouled before he could shoot.
He made the point and the score was 6 to 6.

Five minutes of the quarter had passed when the
Iron Men put in the next goal, and Brent asked for
time out. "Joe," he said, "you take over at guard for
Ben. Thornton, give Gino a rest. Don't let 'em scare
you with that hard charging. Get the ball and wait for
good shots."

They worked it down carefully and fed to the California boy, who scored with a long one-hand jump. As
usual, the Steelville team came tearing down-court,
yelling to each other like Indians. The ball took a long
bounce on the dribble and went right into Pulaski's
big hands as the attacker crashed into him. It knocked
the wind out of the Steelville player while Joe stayed
on his feet.

"Foul!" screamed the Iron Men's partisans. "Block-
ing!"

But the referee ruled otherwise. "Charging," he announced. "The foul is on number three. One and one."

Joe helped his opponent up and went to the penalty
line, grinning happily. He drew a great lungful of air,
sighted at the rim and sank the shot.

The two teams swapped goals twice more before the
period ended, and the Hornets made good on one addi-
tional foul. They led 14 to 12 when they left the floor.
After the brief rest Brent sent Peewee in for Donovan

and moved Joe to center, with Ray Jones taking over the guard spot.

Ray's trouble all year had been careless ball handling. He had improved during the final week of practice, but the period was hardly under way when he let a pass get by him. It went out of bounds and the gray team had the throw-in.

Peewee saw a Steelville man loose in the corner and cut over at full speed to guard him in case of a long pass. It came, just as he expected. The little forward leaped as high as he could, tipping the ball with his fingers, and it bounced crazily to the right. Thornton was there to grab it. He soloed half the length of the floor before the defense could get in front of him, then back-handed to Peewee. The redhead crouched, jumped and let fly with a thirty-foot set shot that skimmed in like a swallow.

The Iron Men, behind now by four points, settled down to steadier basketball. They fed their huge center for two field goals, and on the second Joe Pulaski fouled him as he shot. The try was good. Steelville went out in front again.

For the rest of the half neither team was able to get much of a lead. Try as he would, Joe couldn't quite match his tall opponent on rebounds, and all that kept the Hornets in the running was the work of the second-string forwards. Thornton was shooting with uncanny accuracy, caging more than half his shots. And Pee-

wee's speed and faking took him under the basket twice
for tricky lay-ups. They wound up the half with Steelville only a point ahead, at 28 to 27.

Brent checked on their condition carefully during
the intermission. Ben Greenbaum had recovered from
his collision and was ready to go. None of the rest
showed any signs of weariness, though the durable captain had played the full sixteen minutes.

"I'm going to give you a breather, Johnny," the
coach told him. "We may need you in the last quarter,
so sit this one out. Ben, you go back in with Ray at
guard. Clem, Gino and Jerry start, too. That hot center
of theirs has three personals against him. Maybe you
can tease him into a couple more. That's your specialty,
Gino."

The Italian boy grinned. "I've been watching him,"
he replied. "He's a little careless, waving those long
arms around."

Steelville got the tap and scored first as the third
quarter started. A moment later Gino cut in toward
the basket, feinted temptingly under the towering center's guard, and shot just as the big arm came down. A
prompt whistle stopped the play before the ball hit the
rim, and the referee pointed at the center.

"Hacking," he called. "Two shots."

Gino took his time at the line. His first try bobbled
a little but went in. The second missed and rolled off

the rim to the left where Clem was waiting. His quick lay-up tied the score at 30-all.

The Steelville coach called time at that point and when his team returned there was a new center, shorter and less effective than the other had been. Brent saw the move from the bench and told the Hornets to feed Clem. It worked beautifully. The big pivot man handled his fresh opponent with ease and dropped in a pair of shots before the Iron Men realized what was happening. Hackersville stayed ahead through the quarter and went into the final period with a 39 to 34 lead.

"I said I'd use all of you," Brent told them. "Thornton, go in at center. Jones and Cooley take over the guard spots. Peewee and Jim Hoskins at forward."

It was the first time Cooley and Hoskins had been in a game for weeks, and before the big crowd they were nervous.

The Hornets brought the ball down on offense and worked it carefully around the ring, looking for a break. As Jim Hoskins took a pass someone in the stands yelled "Shoot!" He reacted with a wild toss that missed the backboard and went into the crowd, to the accompaniment of loud whoops from the Steelville rooters.

"That's nothing to worry about, Jim. Don't let 'em rattle you," Peewee told his scarlet-faced friend. But the damage was done. The Iron Men roared down-floor

and the huge center, now back in the line-up, hung up
a goal.

Hoskins clenched his teeth and set out to redeem
himself. The crowd made it as tough for him as possible. Every time he got the ball in the pattern a con-
certed howl went up—"Shoot! Shoot!" But he kept his

head and handled the ball like a veteran. It was a well-timed pass from him to Sedgely in the pivot that put the Hornets back in the scoring column. For once the big Steelville center was off balance, and Thornton spun his one-hander in.

The hard-charging Iron Men were fighting the clock now. They pulled up within one point of the Hornets and the crowd responded with wave on wave of cheers. With four minutes still to play, Peewee cut for the basket and a huge foot tripped him. As he went sprawling he heard the sharp blast of the whistle. He looked up in time to see the giant center raise his hand and ramble dejectedly toward the bench. Unhurt, Peewee stood on the foul line and cut the cords for his eleventh point of the game and the forty-fourth for Hackersville.

Brent chose that moment to send in his fresh first-stringers. They could smell victory now, just as the Iron Men could sense defeat. Clem took a wild shot off the backboard, passed out to Jerry, and the Irish flash was away on a fast break to put them in front by four. After that, with the three-minute rule in effect, all they had to do was hold onto the ball and let the desperate Steelville team foul itself deeper and deeper into the hole. The final score was 57 to 46 and the Hornets were taking it easy at the finish.

A voice on the loud-speaker system pleaded with people to keep their seats, but it was no use. The Hackersville crowd surged down on the floor, hugging the Hornet players, lifting Elmer Brent to their shoulders. Dotty Gordon and the other cheer-leaders pranced out at the head of the band, and the whole Hackersville contingent went into a snake dance.

As soon as they could pull free the squad hurried down the ramp to the locker-room. They wanted to get dressed and watch the second game.

"How do you feel?" Brent asked each of them in turn. "Pretty tired?"

"Gosh, no!" . . . "Fresh as a daisy!" . . . "I could start another game right now," came the answers.

"Okay," he decided. "I guess it won't hurt you to sit through this other semi-final. Watch how the players work. You'll be facing one of these teams tonight."

The Hackersville rooters made room for them in their section of the stand, and they were all settled by the time the two fives squared off. The Franklin team was familiar to all of them. Peewee remembered the lanky center, Lukatz, and Bailey and Craig and Buffo. But it was the Bellwood Bombers, in their sky-blue uniforms, who commanded most of his attention.

They weren't as big as some teams he had seen, but they were all long and lean and looked race-horse fast. As soon as the game started something else was apparent. Their teamwork was as smooth as silk. Franklin got the tap, but the Bomber center took the ball off the backboard on the first try and half a dozen fast passes wound up in a basket. From then on they pulled steadily ahead. Their shooting wasn't spectacular—all their shots seemed to be easy ones—but they kept on scoring. One man accounted for half the goals they made in the first two periods. He was a slender, good-looking youngster named Masterson, and most of his shots were one-hand hooks from about fifteen feet out.

At the end of the half Bellwood led by 32 to 20. The big city fans who made up most of the crowd were stunned. They had expected the Metropolitan champs to have a fairly easy time with the up-state five, and they couldn't believe what they were seeing was true.

Under cover of the band music and the chatter that took place during the intermission, the Hornet squad huddled, heads close together, and talked over what they had seen.

"Looks like that Masterson boy's the one we'll have to stop," said Johnny Gale. "Got any ideas?"

"Yes," Ben answered. "Those Franklin guards are suckers for the Bellwood offense. They get faked out o' position every time, an' all of a sudden he's got the ball with a clear shot. Maybe they'll wise up, this next half."

"I noticed something," Peewee put in. "He's right-handed. All those pretty one-handers are fired from the same spot, over on the right o' the foul line. If he had to go to his left I bet he'd miss."

"That's right," Clem nodded. "Or if somebody pushed their pattern back a couple o' feet he mightn't be able to hit so sweet."

Evidently the Franklin coach had made some of the same observations, for the Tech defense was tighter in the second half. Bellwood tried to use the smooth pattern that had worked so well earlier and ran into trouble. Twice the quick little Italian, Buffo, broke up passes and stole the ball. Another time when Masterson got it in his favorite spot he found Lukatz towering in front of him and had to pass off to one of his team-mates.

Gradually Franklin narrowed the gap. They went into the last three minutes only five points behind. But the Bombers put on a freeze and the Tech cause was lost. To get the ball they had to commit fouls, and the Bellwood penalty shooting was too good. The final score was Bombers, 47, Franklin Tech, 45.

CHAPTER 19

WHEN PEEWEE came back to the Field House at seven, most of the squad was already there. Brent had transformed one end of the dressing room with wrestling mats, covered by blankets.

"Come over and lie down," he told his charges. "Just stretch out there and rest. Take a nap if you feel like it. But anyway, relax."

The place was warm and quiet and nobody felt like talking. Peewee was sleeping like a baby when the coach roused them at the end of half an hour.

"All right, gang," Brent laughed. "Rise and shine— time to get into your togs."

While they undressed and put on their suits he talked to them. He talked about the offensive plays they had practiced all season and the clean, smooth timing that would make them work. He mentioned Masterson and analyzed the defense that had held his scoring down in the second half of the Tech game.

"Johnny and Ben know what to do about him," Brent concluded. "We'll start the first string as usual, and switch forwards at the quarter. That system has been working and I'm going to stay with it. The last half will be tough for both teams but I know you're all in good condition. We'll try to outlast 'em. Get the jump if you can, and never let up. Good luck to you, boys!"

The fluttery feeling was back in Peewee's stomach as they went up the ramp, but he knew he'd get over it when the action started. The great arena had been darkened except for a spotlight on the middle of the floor. Yet it was pulsing with life. The sea of faces went up and up till it was lost in the gloom of the upper tiers. And the noise of the crowd was a low, steady roar like the rumble of surf.

"Wait here," a tournament official told the squad. "When your names are called, each man will dribble the ball out to mid-court, pass it back to the next man and go on across to stand in line. Your team's first. Then, after Bellwood comes out, we'll have the salute to the colors and the national anthem."

There was a long roll of drums and a voice burst from the loud-speakers. "Welcome, folks—welcome to the final game for the State High School championship. We want you to see these young players who have fought their way up through the tournament to this climax game. First we'll introduce the Hornets, from Hackersville—a little up-state school with fewer than a hundred boys but a whale of a basketball team. And here they are! Number one—Captain Johnny Gale!"

The drums rolled again as Johnny trotted out into the bright circle of the spotlight, and the crowd applauded. Ben Greenbaum's name was called, then Clem's, Gino's and Jerry's, in order. Joe Pulaski followed and then it was Peewee's turn. Joe bounced the ball high and he had to jump for it, much to the crowd's delight. The cheers and clapping were loud in his ears as he sprinted out, backhanding to Thornton behind him.

When they were lined up along the far side of the floor, the Bellwood squad was introduced. A color guard marched out next, and the spectators rose while the massed bands played *The Star-spangled Banner*.

Peewee stood very straight, his face solemn. There was something so impressive about the ceremony that he had a choked-up feeling. It made him proud and humble at the same time.

Then the moment was gone. They broke ranks and the two squads ran to opposite ends of the court. For five fast minutes they worked under the hoop, sharpening their ball-handling and shooting. When the whistle blew they went back to the bench.

Peewee gripped the hands of the starting five and wished he could be going out there with them. He was so keyed up he had to hug himself to keep from trembling.

Clem Johnson was facing a center no taller than himself, and on the opening toss he easily outjumped him. Tapped to Ben Greenbaum, the ball went to Jerry, to Gino and in to Clem at the pivot. His hook looked sure and easy but it rimmed the basket without going in. The Bellwood center was there to take it. His forwards went down like lightning and only Johnny was there to try to stem their attack. Masterson got behind him on a quick pass and laid up the first two-pointer of the game.

The Hornet guards brought the ball out methodically, worked it into scoring distance and fed to Jerry, who faked a pass, then cut for the hoop. His quick lay-up missed and Peewee groaned. Was this going to be one of those nights when there was a lid on the basket—when nothing went right?

But in the next second Clem took the rebound. Blocked from a shot, he tossed out to Greenbaum who set himself and arched a bull's-eye through to tie it up. For the first few minutes it looked like a low-scoring game. Both sides were playing cautiously, using tight defenses. Once, in spite of the Hornet guards, Masterson found the range with one of his pretty 15-footers. Once Jerry committed a foul on an attempted steal. A fine pivot shot by Clem Johnson earned two points for Hackersville, and they trailed at 5-4 with three minutes left in the quarter. Before the period ended they traded goals once more, and Gino, fouled while shooting, sank both his penalty points. The Hornets led by 8 to 7 when the whistle sounded.

"I think," Brent told them, "they'll try to step it up this next quarter. They've got the speed and you may see some fast breaking. You fresh forwards had better be prepared to run with 'em. And make those shots count. You only cashed three out of twelve tries in the first period. That's not good enough."

Peewee limbered his legs and drew a deep breath before he reported in. There were none of the usual laughs and jeers when he took the floor. Many of the spectators had been there that afternoon and knew what the small redhead could do.

It was Bellwood's throw-in. There was a long pass, a race for the basket and a looping shot by Masterson that suddenly put the Bombers ahead. Gale brought the ball down quickly and cross-courted to Peewee. He saw the defense was concentrating on Clem, while Thornton was in the clear, and he rifled a pass over to him. The California boy took it and jumped, all in one motion, and his one-hander sailed true—the second score in a quarter of a minute of play!

The furious pace kept up. Clem made a beautiful steal on the throw-in, passed to Ben and sprinted for the basket. As the ball came back to him he laid it up for another two-pointer. Bellwood retaliated with a goal, but the Hornets put on a fast break of their own. A forty-foot pass to Peewee, a solo dash down-floor, and the little forward arched one over the Bomber center's head to make the score 14-11. They had their shooting eyes now. Even the coach couldn't complain about three baskets on three shots.

The Bellwood five continued to feed Masterson, but Johnny and Ben teamed up on him and he was forced to shoot from outside his favorite 15-foot range. He missed twice, and although the center got the rebound and scored on one of his tries, Clem took the other off the boards. Peewee caught the pass, faked a cut and bounced low to Thornton, who made good with another jump shot.

Brent had diagnosed the Bombers' strategy correctly. They forced the pace constantly and the green-shirted five had to run all out to match their speed. Bellwood's shooting showed signs of improvement, too. In spite of all they could do, the Hornets were unable to get more than two or three points ahead, for every time they scored their opponents bounced right back. At the end of the first half they led by a thin 25-to-23 margin.

Back in the dressing room Brent wasted no time in words. His boys were tired and he spent every minute rubbing their legs and arms. All he said when they returned to the floor was, "Stay with 'em, gang. Remem-

ber—they're just as bushed as you are. And keep the pressure on that star o' theirs."

He sent in the same line-up that had started, with a single change. Pulaski replaced Clem, who looked as if he needed a rest.

The strain of playing two games in a day began to tell in that third period. Bellwood started a whole new team, apparently as fast as the first one. They moved the ball well but had trouble getting the range, and the panting Hornets succeeded in holding them, goal for goal, through the opening minutes. Then the Bombers broke the game wide open. A steal and a fast break gave them two quick points, and a foul by the exasperated Jerry Donovan put them in the lead at 32 to 31. A moment later Joe was whistled down for charging, and another point went into the basket.

Gino managed to tie it up with a hook shot but Bellwood came right back with a lay-up from the pivot. Brent was up and pacing back and forth, his hands deep in his pockets. With a minute to go the Bombers still held a two-point lead and they stretched it to three on another Donovan foul before the period ended.

They were going into the home stretch now. This final quarter was the pay-off. Elmer Brent looked at the drawn faces and heaving chests of his weary team and tried to find a combination that could go down to the wire. Ben Greenbaum was about done. Johnny Gale was rugged and might last. Clem and the second-string forwards had had some rest. The coach dropped Joe Pulaski back to Ben's guard post and sent them out with a hope and a prayer.

It was the Hornets' ball. Johnny tossed out to Joe and the big Polish boy galloped down the sideline. A Bellwood guard deliberately got in his way, trying to draw him into another charging foul, but the referee called it a block. Joe went to the line, ready to do or die. His first try was too strong and bounced clear back to him. On the second he steadied himself and put it in.

Masterson was playing again, and before Johnny and Joe could get their defense organized he made his presence felt with a floating push shot that sailed through. The score was 40 to 36. A few people in the cheering crowd seemed to think it was all over, for there was restless movement in the stands. Peewee didn't notice it. All he knew was that they had to get back those points.

He had the ball on Johnny's pass, and by some miracle of dodging and twisting he threaded his way through the defense. Twenty feet from the basket there was one big man still in front of him, pressing him hard. He eye-faked to the left, cut to the right and went up in a desperate jump as the guard slapped at his arm. For a slow second the ball hung on the rim. Then it dropped through and the whistle came simultaneously.

"The goal counts," snapped the referee. "Hacking on Number Eight. One shot plus one."

Peewee wiped the sweat out of his eyes and waited for the players to take their positions along the foul lane. His arms felt dead, but he knew he must sink this one. It bobbled in on the first try and the cheers

rose to a deafening pitch. The fans who had started
to leave sat down again.

There was no let-down in the pace of that nightmare
quarter. Fresh reserves came in for Bellwood. They
kept the pressure on and all the Hornets could do was
fight back doggedly. They ran with the Bombers stride
for stride in spite of leaden feet and aching lungs, and
held them even with their shooting.

When the officials announced there were three minutes to go, the score was 44 to 43 in Bellwood's favor.

"They'll freeze it now," Johnny Gale gasped. "Get
the ball if you can but try not to foul."

The Bombers must have had a lot of practice in
controlling the ball for that was the tightest freeze
Peewee had ever seen. His despair grew deeper as the
scoreless seconds ticked away. Joe Pulaski made a lunge
to intercept a pass and though he tried to avoid it, his
shoulder jarred against Masterson. The young star
stepped coolly to the line and dropped in his first try.
The second was a fraction of an inch too far to the
right. As it fell off the rim Clem Johnson made a magnificent leap and grabbed it.

With just over a minute to go, Bellwood led by two
points. But the Hornets had the ball. They broke
through an all-court press and set up their play. At
the center of the weaving pattern was Clem, waving
his arms in the pivot spot, drawing attention to himself.

236

"Here!" he yelled hoarsely and at the signal Peewee flipped the ball to Thornton. The tall boy's jump was jerky but his aim was good. As the one-hander dropped in a tremendous roar went up from the crowd. The score was deadlocked and there were only thirty seconds left.

The Bombers brought the ball down with calculated slowness, making their passes short and sure, as if they wanted the game to go into overtime. Peewee stole a glance at the big clock. Twenty seconds—fifteen seconds. He saw Masterson waiting at the fifteen-foot mark and knew in a flash what was going to happen. If only he could time it right. He edged a little nearer to the Bellwood star and when the pass came—the pass that was supposed to win the game, he jumped with all the strength he had left. His fingers tipped the ball. There it was, bouncing just in front of him. All he had to do was reach out for it, dribble the length of the floor and shoot a basket. The first few strides went all right. Then he knew his legs wouldn't carry him any farther.

Dizzily he saw Clem a few yards away, and managed to heave the ball in his direction. Then he stumbled to his knees. Through blurred eyes he watched the knot of players converging on the basket. A long brown arm shot up and the ball swished through the cords just as the gun went off.

CHAPTER 20

THERE MAY have been wilder finishes to a State Championship than that one, but nobody in the big crowd had ever seen it happen. For the next ten minutes complete pandemonium rocked the Field House.

Before he knew it Peewee was hoisted bodily off the floor and perched on the shoulders of the howling mob. Girls he had never seen before reached up and tried to hug him. He caught a glimpse of his mother a little way off in the throng and saw the worry in her face.

"Hey—let me down!" he croaked. "It's my mom! I've got to tell her I'm all right!"

But nobody heard him and all he could do was wave at her and grin.

At last the frenzy began to subside. The stranger who

was carrying Peewee set him down with a pat on the head and he made his way stiffly down the ramp to the locker-room.

Most of the others were already there. "Yea, Sparky!" they yelled in chorus as he came in. "What a game, boy! What a play! Wow!"

Brent motioned him to a bench. "Lie down," he commanded. "Let me get the kinks out o' those legs."

Half an hour later, showered, dressed and smelling strongly of liniment, the squad left the scene of their triumph. The stars were out and it was a fine spring night. Wearily but blissfully they got into their families' cars and headed for home.

Peewee couldn't remember when he had slept as late as he did that Sunday. Bone-tired, he had fallen into bed and gone to sleep instantly. At eleven in the morning the church bells woke him but he turned over and slept some more. When he finally came downstairs his mother was getting dinner and his father sat happily in the living room surrounded by sections of the Sunday papers.

"Well, Son," he chuckled, "there's plenty about Hackersville in the sports pages this morning. Want to see what they say about you? Listen to this headline— 'Pocket-size Basketeer Puts Sting in Hornets.' And this —'A red-headed flash who stands knee-high to a grasshopper turned defeat into victory in the State Championship final last night.' "

Peewee made a face. "Hold it, Dad," he said. "I'd rather not hear the stuff. Brent sort of cured us of reading about ourselves. All I want to know is, did we really win? I was afraid I'd dreamed it."

Thornton Sedgely came over that afternoon. "I had to get away," he laughed. "My dad heard the game on the radio last night and he's been telling it back to me —every play. Mother says he nearly had apoplexy, those last few minutes. It must have sounded like a thriller, at that. I'll never know how you intercepted that pass to Masterson. You must have been four feet off the floor when you touched it!"

"Did you boys hear about the party the Chamber of Commerce is going to throw?" Mr. Carson put in. "They say you've put Hackersville on the map, so they're having a testimonial dinner next Friday night in the hotel ballroom. Too bad," he added mischievously, "but I guess you'll all have to make speeches."

The idea horrified Peewee. He went around most of the week wondering how he could catch the mumps or some other disease that would keep him out of the affair. Finally Johnny Gale relieved his mind.

"Speeches are out," he announced firmly. "We'll be introduced—sure. But nobody has to say more than a couple o' words."

That week's issue of the *Clarion* was devoted almost exclusively to the basketball team and its accomplishments. But there was one item on the front page that made Peewee's eyes pop.

It was headed "Engagement Announced," and it went on to say that "Mr. and Mrs. Frederick G. Carson, of Elm Street, announce the engagement of their daughter, Jane Anne, to Elmer Forrest Brent, coach of the Hackersville High School basketball team." There was more of it, covering the young couple's educational background, and the piece concluded with the information that the wedding would take place in June.

"Hey, Mom!" Peewee yelled. "When did all this happen—Jane and Elmer Brent, I mean?"

His mother beamed. "You were too busy with basketball to notice what was going on," she told him. "What do you think of it?"

"Gosh," he said, trying to adjust to the new idea, "I guess it's okay—sure, I guess it's better'n that—it's swell!"

*　　*　　*

Friday night came, and four hundred people jammed the modest ballroom of the hotel. The basketball squad, dressed in their best Sunday suits, sat uncomfortably at the head table, flanked by the coach and the toastmaster. Just in front of them were the cheer-leaders and the band. Dotty Gordon looked up at Peewee and winked solemnly.

In contrast to the team, the townspeople were in a gala mood. They talked, laughed and sang throughout the meal. It was a pretty good dinner and Joe Pulaski and a few others did full justice to it while Peewee toyed with his food.

Finally the dessert dishes were cleared away and the toastmaster pounded the table for silence. He rose and cleared his throat.

"Hackersville has a right to be proud tonight," he began in ringing tones. For twenty minutes he continued in that vein, showering the team with oratorical bouquets. The boys squirmed and fidgeted.

"And now," the speaker wound up with a flourish, "I wish to present to you the man who has done more than any other to make our town famous—our blushing bridegroom-to-be—our own great coach—Elmer Brent!"

Brent wasn't blushing when he got to his feet. He looked pale but composed.

"Thank you, Mr. Toastmaster and good friends," he said. "I'm not going to make any speech, but I want to say it wasn't any miracle of coaching that made this team a winner. It was a bunch of kids with courage and heart. Go as strong as you like in praising them. They deserve every word of it. And there's one more thing I think I ought to tell you folks. This week I've had two offers of college coaching jobs. More money, of course, and more prestige. It's a pretty big temptation to a young man about to be married."

He waited a moment, while the exclamations of distress quieted down. "I'm going to refuse those bids," he went on. "That's because I know I was lucky this year, with a veteran team to build on. Three of those regulars are graduating in June. If I left now I'd never be sure how much I'd been able to contribute to the championship. We may not have as good a record next year, but I'd like to prove to Hackersville and myself that we can win games with the material that's left. So I'm staying here at least one more season."

A spontaneous cheer went up all over the room and the happy crowd continued clapping for a full minute after he sat down.

The toastmaster called for order again. "All of us," he said, "are mighty glad you've made that decision, Mr. Brent. We didn't know about the college bids, but maybe this will help. The businessmen of Hackersville have raised enough money this week to buy a building lot for you, and here's an added check for five hundred dollars to help you start a home. It's a sort of wedding present to you and the future Mrs. Brent."

Peewee was watching Jane where she sat with her parents. She was dabbing her eyes with a handkerchief but he had never seen her look so pretty.

"And now for the team," the toastmaster announced, when the coach had expressed his thanks for the check. "Everybody here knows these young men. You've seen them play. You've cheered for them till you were hoarse. We don't expect speeches but we'd like each one to say something. First I give you the Hornets'

stalwart captain and four-year letter man—Johnny
Gale!"

One after another, as the introductions were made,
they stood up, mumbled a few words and sat down.
Peewee sat at the end of the row, growing more and
more uneasy as his turn approached.

"All right, folks," said the toastmaster with a grin,
"let's have a big hand. Last and smallest, but far from
least—Gregory Carson, sparkplug of the Hornets!"

Somehow the boy found himself on his feet. He
tried to speak but the applause drowned him out.
Then from a corner of the room came a shout. "We
want to know how tall he is. Tell us, Sparky!"

Peewee reddened. When he could make himself heard he gave them some news.

"Last fall," he said, "when I came out for the team, I guess I was a shrimp, all right. No matter how hard I tried to make myself bigger, five feet three was the best I could do."

He had to wait while the crowd laughed and applauded. "But," he went on triumphantly, "believe it or not I've grown this winter. I hadn't measured myself for three months until yesterday, and now I'm five, four and three-quarters in my sox!"

He sat down to a great roar of cheers and handclaps, and in a few moments the affair was over. Outside, under the cool night sky, Thornton and Peewee started homeward.

"You were terrific," laughed the California boy. "That speech of yours was the hit of the whole evening. Only, for Pete's sake, Peewee, don't grow too much! How are you going to run under those long-legged guards if you're six feet tall?"

Peewee grinned. "I wouldn't worry about that," he said. "I know I'll always be pint-sized. But after all, Johnny O'Brien and a couple of other small guys have done all right!"